Hiya . . .

Of all the sisters in the Chocolate Box Girls series, Honey is the one who fascinates me the most. Is she mean, manipulative and out of control or is there a lost, broken little girl hidden away behind the tough-kid mask? The more I wrote, the more certain I was that it was the latter.

Sent to stay with her dad in Australia, Honey is trying hard to turn over a new leaf. Her new life in the sun isn't quite what she expected, but it has some bright points: new friends Bennie and Tara, surf boy Riley and cool, kind cafe boy Ash. But can Honey really trust her new friends? When things begin to unravel and she finds herself in the middle of a nightmare, who can she turn to?

Sweet Honey is a story of new beginnings, of friendship, trust and falling in love . . . but also a story of cyber-bullying, stalking and falling apart.

Sometimes, you have to let go of the past to move on, to fall to pieces before you can begin putting yourself back together. And, sometimes, a family can hide a secret that changes everything.

Sweet Honey has all the drama you'd expect from the most outrageous Tanberry sister, but expect the unexpected too . . . and enjoy!

Cathy Cassidy

Sweet Honey

the chocolate box girls

PUFFIN

PUFFIN BOOKS

UK | USA | Canada | Ireland | Australia
India | New Zealand | South Africa

Puffin Books is part of the Penguin Random House group of companies
whose addresses can be found at global.penguinrandomhouse.com.

puffinbooks.com

First published 2014
Published in this edition 2015
001

Text copyright © Cathy Cassidy, 2014
Illustrations copyright © Puffin Books, 2014
Illustrations by Sara Chadwick-Holmes
All rights reserved

The moral right of the author and illustrator has been asserted

Set in Baskerville MT Std
Typeset by Palimpsest Book Production Limited, Falkirk, Stirlingshire
Printed in Great Britain by Clays Ltd, St Ives plc

British Library Cataloguing in Publication Data
A CIP catalogue record for this book is available from the British Library

ISBN: 978-0-141-34163-7

www.greenpenguin.co.uk

Penguin Random House is committed to a
sustainable future for our business, our readers
and our planet. This book is made from Forest
Stewardship Council® certified paper.

Thanks . . .

To Liam, Cal and Cait for being awesome, and to Mum, Joan, Andy, Lori and all my brilliant family for putting up with me! Thanks to Helen, Sheena, Fiona, Mary-Jane, Maggi, Lal, Mel, Jessie, Jan and all my lovely friends for always being there with support, chocolate and hugs.

Thanks to Ruth, my PA; Martyn, who does the sums; Annie for her help with the tours; and of course to Darley and his angels for being amazing. Hugs to Amanda, my ever-patient editor, and to Sara for the gorgeous artwork. Thanks also to Adele, Tanya, Emily, Julia, Carolyn, Jess, Samantha, Helen and all at Puffin.

Thanks to Mo, Kate, Sara and any Aussie readers who helped refresh my memory and answer my questions about Sydney . . . and to YOU, my fab readers far and wide, for your enthusiasm, loyalty and support. You're the best . . . end of story.

Dear Honey,

If you're reading this note you are probably at the
departure gate or maybe actually up in the clouds
already, on the way to Australia. It's just to say some
of the things I couldn't say out loud. I didn't want to
cry, and I didn't want us to argue. So here goes.

A. You may be the most annoying big sister in the world,
but I am going to miss you.

B. I know it's not forever but I think you are making a
BIG mistake. It is bad enough having a dad on the
other side of the planet without losing your sister too.

C. Things won't be the same without you. (They will
probably be a lot quieter, but I don't care, I still wish
you weren't going.)

Your favourite Sister,
Coco xxx

1

I smile and fold the note neatly, putting it back into the pocket of my shoulder bag. My little sister is crazy, and I will miss her too, but she knows as well as I do that my days at Tanglewood are over. I've messed up one time too many. What can I say? Getting a friend to hack into the school computer system to fake my grades and school reports was not my best move, and getting caught and expelled kind of sealed the deal.

I needed a one-way ticket out of there, and Dad stepped up to the mark and provided me with one – a ticket to Australia, a new start, a way out of the mess my life has been lately. Who wouldn't have said yes?

It takes twenty-three hours to fly from London Heathrow to Sydney, and that is a very long time to be stuck in cattle-class on a plane. I eat the weird, pre-packed dinner on a tray and ask for a glass of wine to go with it, but the stewardess just rolls her eyes and hands me an orange juice. Everything tastes of sawdust anyway, so I don't much care. We stop off in Singapore for the plane to refuel, but apart from a brief walk around the airport I don't get to actually see anything of the place. And then we're back on the plane and the other passengers yawn and tip their seats back and huddle down under thin fleece blankets with funny little eye-masks on, and the lights go down on life as I know it.

I am too excited to sleep. Australia – land of sunshine, surf, opportunities! I take out a pocket sketchbook and doodle pictures of myself flying through the stars, wearing a sundress and feathered wings and my vintage high-heeled boots.

I put on my headphones and watch two movies in a row; then I flick on my overhead light and read two magazines. Like I said, it's a long flight. I go to the bathroom and walk up and down the aisle for exercise a few times like they tell you to do on long-haul flights, but the eye-rolly stewardess gives me a very sour look, so I sit down again and try to be patient.

Maybe I actually do fall asleep, for a minute or two at least, because the next thing I know, the lights snap on again

❀❀❀❀❀❀❀❀❀❀❀❀❀❀❀❀❀❀❀❀❀❀❀❀

and the sky outside is pink with the promise of dawn. It's almost morning, Sydney time. The stewardess hands me a sawdust-flavoured, shrink-wrapped breakfast but I am so excited I can't eat a thing, and then we are buckling up the seat belts ready for landing. Finally.

When I walk out on to those aeroplane steps and take my first ever look at a Sydney daybreak, I am so brimful of happiness I think I might burst.

Dad is waiting for me at Arrivals, tanned and smiling, effortlessly cool in a grey linen suit. He has to be forty, easily, but he doesn't look it. As always, he draws a few admiring glances from women of a certain age, but Dad's grin is all for me. I run towards him, pulling my wheely suitcase behind me, and he scoops me up in a big bear hug, laughing.

'How's my best girl?' he asks, and I am so happy I could burst. I've waited a very long time to hear those words.

'Breakfast?' he suggests, swinging up my heavy suitcase as if it weighs nothing. 'Those flights are a killer and plane food is the pits. Let's get you something decent!'

Having eaten almost nothing on the plane, I am suddenly starving. I follow Dad into the leafy enclosure of an upmarket

❀❀❀❀❀❀❀❀❀❀❀❀❀❀❀❀❀❀❀❀❀❀❀

airport restaurant, and he orders for both of us, something fancy with poached eggs and hollandaise sauce, freshly squeezed orange juice, croissants, jam.

'So,' he says, leaning back as the waitress hurries off with our order. 'Here we go. A new start in Australia! What's going on, Honey Tanberry?'

I raise my chin. I have messed up, I know it. I have made so many mistakes it's hard to know where to begin. It started with me skipping school, telling lies, staying out all night with a fairground boy called Kes and his unsuitable friends. Mum was majorly upset about that, and I was glad. Yes, Kes was older than me; yes, he was trouble. So what? I happen to like trouble.

I am good at it too. You could say I have trouble down to a fine art. I lied, I cheated, I stopped studying. Then came the bit I mentioned, about persuading a friend to hack the school computer system and 'adjust' my grades. We got found out. I ended up with social services on my case, with Mum crying and my sisters yelling and my stupid stepdad Paddy raking a hand through his hair and looking at me sadly as if I was the one who pulled our happy family to bits, and not him.

4

Yeah, well, we all know that isn't how it happened.

It doesn't matter because in the end I've got what I wanted – the fresh start to beat them all. A new life, with Dad, in Australia.

I have done my research. I know that Australia is beautiful, sunshiny, unspoilt. It's the perfect place for new beginnings. It's also the place where Britain once shipped its convicts, long ago.

I reckon I will fit right in.

'I take it you were struggling, living with your mum?' Dad says, sipping a latte. 'Not all happy families, huh?'

'We haven't been a family for ages,' I tell him flatly. 'Not since you left.'

Dad just laughs, but it's true. He knows I don't blame him – it's what happened afterwards that did the damage.

When Dad left, that whole family thing slipped through our fingers and shattered like glass. We tried to pick up the pieces, put them together again, but we just couldn't. The only one who could have done it was Dad, and before he got the chance Paddy pitched up with his hateful, boyfriend-stealing daughter Cherry and that was that. Dad took a transfer out to Australia and my dream that

❀❀❀❀❀❀❀❀❀❀❀❀❀❀❀❀❀❀❀❀❀❀❀

he'd come back to us some day bit the dust big style. One broken family, no longer any hope for repairs.

'Life moves on,' Dad says lightly. 'I know I couldn't always be there for you. I can see you've found it tough, these last few years.'

'Just a bit.'

It's not like I didn't try my best – I threw confetti at the wedding, smiled at Paddy across the breakfast table, resisted the urge to slap Cherry's lying, cheating face. I pretended it was all OK, but it wasn't, and sooner or later I knew the game of let's pretend would fall apart.

It all blew up, and things were looking pretty bad – then Dad chucked me a lifeline and here I am, shipped out to Australia, a modern-day convict girl. I will be attending a private school that sounds like a cross between bad-girl boot camp and hippy-dippy wholemeal heaven, with counselling and one-to-one support to help me pass a handful of exams after all.

'Things will be better here,' Dad says. 'A fresh start. You're my girl, Honey – I know you can make a go of it, turn things around. Right?'

'Right!' I agree.

❀❀❀❀❀❀❀❀❀❀❀❀❀❀❀❀❀❀❀❀❀❀❀❀

Well, maybe.

I am just happy to be here, with a clean slate and a last, last chance to get my life on track. I am determined to make it work. Call me cynical, but sometimes it is easier to walk away from a messed-up life than to stick around and patch things up. It doesn't mean I don't love my mum and sisters – I do. I just can't be a part of the new-look family they've put together.

Fresh starts . . . Dad has always been good at those, and I plan to be too.

'You're a lot like me, you know, Honey,' Dad tells me between mouthfuls of breakfast. 'I was a bit of a rebel in my time. I had a few ups and downs, a few changes of school before I settled. We're alike, you and I.'

I smile. I want to be like Dad – who wouldn't? He is dramatic, confident, charismatic. He has this magic about him – when he looks at you, you feel like you're the only person in the whole wide world. You feel special, chosen, golden.

I felt this way all the time when I was a kid – I was Dad's favourite. Then he left, and everything turned to dust. Without Dad, everything at Tanglewood was cold and empty and hollow.

❀❀❀❀❀❀❀❀❀❀❀❀❀❀❀❀❀❀❀❀❀❀❀

It will be different here.

Dad is telling me about the house, the pool, the nearby beach. He is explaining how Sydney is the most beautiful city he knows, how he will help me explore it, how I will learn to love it too.

I almost miss it when Dad mentions, ever so casually, that it won't be just me and him in the fancy beachside bungalow with the outdoor pool. It will be me, him and his girlfriend, Emma. My ears buzz and for a moment everything seems foggy, cold. It could be jet lag, but I don't think so. Through the fog, Dad's words worm themselves into my brain.

'Emma's lovely,' he says carelessly. 'You'll get along great!'

Emma. The name rings a bell, but I think it's just the situation that's familiar. Disappointment curdles in my belly, sharp and sour. I have spent years without my dad, and I really, really don't want to share him now.

It looks as if I have flown halfway round the world to escape an annoying stepdad, only to have acquired some kind of stepmum.

That was never part of the plan.

Cherry Costello
<cherryblossomgirl@chocolatebox.co.uk>
to me ✉

Hope you've landed safely. It's weird, the house
feels all empty and wrong without you. We don't
always see eye to eye, Honey, but I honestly never
wanted us to be enemies. I know you feel that me
and Dad don't belong at Tanglewood, but if you'd
just give us a chance you might change your mind.
I am genuinely sorry for what happened with Shay,
you know that. I hope we can be friends one day.
Cherry xxx

2

Scanning through emails on my phone while Dad pays at the till, I laugh out loud at the sickly sweet message. Friends one day? Seriously, my stepsister has no idea.

I press Delete, but the email reminds me to tread carefully. Making instant enemies out of Paddy Costello and his lying, cheating daughter Cherry may not have been my smartest move ever, but what can I say? I saw them for what they were, a small-time Willie Wonka wannabe and his chancer kid who moved right in and made themselves at home in the life that used to be mine. I told it like it was and my sisters slowly turned against me. Somehow I was the bad guy.

I won't make that mistake again.

I am not wild about the idea of sharing my dad with anyone, but I want my new life in Australia to work. I will

turn on the charm, be sweet and friendly, polite and helpful. I will get along with Emma if it kills me.

When Dad's fancy car with its tinted windows and surround-
sound CD system and sunroof finally draws to a halt outside
their modern villa bungalow, Emma is there on the doorstep, all smiles and suntan and perfectly styled hair. I step
out of the car and she throws her arms round me, saying
how glad she is to meet me. She is younger than Mum, and
she doesn't look like she'd be seen dead baking cakes or
mopping floors or sitting at the kitchen table making lino-
print Christmas cards. Emma looks sleek and manicured.
Her clothes are expensive, tailored, and her gold-hoop
earrings are understated, classy.

She fits with Dad's high-powered life in a way Mum
never did.

'We want you to be happy,' she says, and I realize that
she has an English accent, which jolts me a little. Could
she have come out here with Dad? I push the thought away.

'This is probably very different from what you're used
to,' Emma is saying. 'But it's your home now, and we're
glad to have you here. I hope we can be friends!'

❀❀❀❀❀❀❀❀❀❀❀❀❀❀❀❀❀❀❀❀❀

First Cherry, then Emma . . . what is it with everyone wanting to be my friend all of a sudden? I drag up a polite smile as Emma embarks on a guided tour of the gardens. I trail after her across the patchy lawn as she points out a eucalyptus tree, a few scrubby shrubs and a luxuriant honeysuckle clinging to a garden archway. We step through the archway and round to the back of the house, and I stop short, catching my breath. A long strip of glinting turquoise water lies before me – a swimming pool edged with marbled grey tiles, a couple of sunloungers arranged beside it. I want to slide into the water fully clothed right now, let go of everything, feel my plane-tangled hair float out around me like a halo.

'Like it?' Dad asks. 'Amazing, right? The beach is just a couple of blocks away too. It's not one of the busy ones, but there's a cafe and a lifeguard and safe swimming. We had Christmas dinner there last year . . . champagne and turkey cold cuts in the sunshine.'

'Wow,' I say, trying to get my head around the idea of that.

'Come on,' Emma says. 'Let's show you inside, get you settled.'

❀❀❀❀❀❀❀❀❀❀❀❀❀❀❀❀❀❀❀❀❀❀

The house is much smaller than Tanglewood, obviously, and it's bright, airy, minimalist. I like that; I want to wipe out the past, start everything fresh. My bedroom doesn't have the character of my turret room back home, but the walls are newly whitewashed and there's a small TV, a kettle and a mini-fridge. It's like a student bedsit and I have my own en suite shower room, which is pure luxury after the chaos of sharing with four stressy sisters, Mum and Paddy. At Tanglewood, only the B&B guests have their own bathrooms.

'Take your time, freshen up a bit,' Dad suggests. 'Once you're sorted, we'll go out and take a look around Sydney, show you the sights, do the whole tourist bit . . .'

The long flight is starting to catch up with me and I'd rather curl up and sleep for a week, but I push the thought away. 'Sure!' I say brightly. 'Cool!'

'That's my girl,' he says approvingly. 'Never give in to jet lag. You have to adapt from the very start to the new time zone, or your body clock will be all over the place. I've taken a couple of days off work; let's not waste them!'

An hour later I am showered and changed, my hair flying out behind me as Dad drives the three of us into the heart of the city with the roof of his car opened up to catch the sun. We park beside the skyscraper office block where his agency is based, just a stone's throw from the botanical gardens and Sydney Cove.

'This is where I work,' he tells me casually, nodding up towards the shiny-sleek building. 'We're on the fifth floor. I'm run off my feet usually – ask Emma, she hardly ever sees me. I can always find time for my beautiful daughter, though – we'll do lunch some time, shall we?'

'OK!' I grin.

'As long as you book him a week or so ahead,' Emma says. 'He works long hours!'

Dad laughs. 'Hey, the money has to come from some-where! C'mon, Emma, you can't call me a workaholic – I've taken time off to help Honey settle in, haven't I?'

'You have indeed,' Emma agrees, and my cheeks glow pink with pleasure. I feel valued, wanted, loved. Finally.

Dad grins. 'Well, I'll resist the temptation to call in and see how they're coping without me. How about we show you this beautiful city?'

We walk through the Royal Botanical Gardens, past the flower gardens and fountains, with the sun beating down on us, white cockatoos squawking overhead and fruit bats hanging from the branches of the trees. It doesn't quite feel real, as if I might wake up at any moment and find I'm back home at Tanglewood with the same old family madness going on around me. Instead I am here, with Sydney Harbour spread out before me like a present I've wanted all my life and hardly dare to open.

I stop for a moment just to pinch myself and to soak up the view as we head down to Circular Quay. We walk round the famous opera house with its roof that looks like gigantic folded wings, and I hand Emma my camera and ask her to take some pictures of Dad and me in front of it, tourist style. I get pictures of some cool Aboriginal guys wearing bodypaint and not much else, playing didgeridoo for the tourists at the quayside; I photograph the amazing Sydney Harbour Bridge, and Dad points out the tiny figures making their way along the curving arc of it; we catch a ferry, and I photograph the churning water, the blue sky, the sweeping curves of Sydney Cove. At Manly, I photograph shark nets on the beach, lifeguard lookout towers, bright boulevards busy with schoolkids trailing home from class in peaked caps and cut-off shorts, streaks of zinc sunblock striped across their cheeks. On the walkway teenagers shoot past on rollerblades, and a young man with a surfboard and blond dreadlocks walks down to the water's edge and paddles his board into the waves, while tanned girls in tiny bikinis play volleyball in the sand.

If that's not surreal enough, I notice strings of fairy lights draped from the trees and a giant artificial Christmas tree in one of the main shopping areas. Piped Christmas carols drift out from one of the shops. It's the end of November and the heat is tropical, but hey, you can't stop Christmas.

Later, back at Circular Quay, we eat dinner and sit looking out across the harbour. Emma and I choose salad and potato wedges and Dad tucks into a kangaroo steak, which seems pretty gross to me, but I don't say so. It's lucky my little sister Coco can't see him. We sip white wine spritzers – even me because Dad says I am pretty grown-up now, and the wine is watered down so it's no big deal. It makes me feel good that Dad and Emma are treating me as an adult; I know for a fact that Mum would have ordered me lemonade.

'So,' Dad says. 'What d'you think, Honey? Ready for a new start in beautiful Sydney?'

❀❀❀❀❀❀❀❀❀❀❀❀❀❀❀❀❀❀❀❀❀❀❀❀

'Totally,' I say. 'I love it already!'

He shrugs. 'Well, it's not just about loving it. It's about making a go of it. We're giving you a fresh start here – are you up for the challenge?'

The smile slips from my face. 'Of course,' I say. 'You know I am. I'll change, I promise. I've been unhappy, mixed up, a little bit off the rails . . .'

'Time to grow up,' Dad says firmly. 'Draw a line under the mistakes. We're taking a risk, Honey, having you here. Don't let us down.'

'I won't!'

I have spent the last couple of years messing up, but if Dad had still been around I'd never have dared step out of line. I was unhappy, lashing out, but all that is behind me now. I've moved on. My transformation from convict girl to all-star Aussie student is about to begin.

'A few rules,' Dad says. 'No boys, no parties, no trouble. Deal?'

'Deal,' I echo. I didn't expect rules or demands from Dad, but I know I don't want to let him down. I know I have to change if I'm going to make a success of my new start in Australia.

❀❀❀❀❀❀❀❀❀❀❀❀❀❀❀❀❀❀❀❀❀❀❀

'I can do it,' I promise. 'How can I fail? This new progressive school you and Mum found sounds amazing. I know I'll need help to turn things around, but Kember Grange offers that, right? It sounds perfect!'

Dad frowns. 'About that. We had a slight change of plan.'

I blink, and Emma shakes her head, refusing to catch my eye. 'You didn't tell her?' she asks. 'Greg, we agreed . . .'

'I didn't want to worry Charlotte.' Dad shrugs, dismissing Emma's comment. 'Our plans changed a little at the last minute, Honey, but I had the impression you were keen to come out here no matter what. Was I right?'

Panic unfurls inside me, but I try to seem calm. 'You were right,' I say. 'So . . . I'm not going to the progressive school after all? What happened?'

Dad leans back in his chair. 'Your mum was very set on that place. She seems to think you need counselling and kid-glove treatment, but I disagree. You're my daughter – you're bright, confident, clued-up – why would you need all that New Age nonsense?'

Because I'm lost, a small voice says inside of me. *I'm lost and I'm not sure I can find myself again.*

'Mum always exaggerates,' I say out loud. 'I'm fine!'

'Kember Grange couldn't fit you in as a day-pupil this term,' Emma explains. 'I don't know if you're aware, but here in Australia the school year ends in December. There's a break for the summer holidays – just imagine, summer in January – then the new term begins. We might be able to secure a place for you then . . .'

'But it's not practical to keep you out of school until the end of January,' Dad chips in. 'You've missed enough schooling as it is. You need to get back to classes as soon as possible, and the last thing you need is a bunch of counsellors on your tail, asking how you feel every step of the way. You don't need therapy; you need discipline and routine!'

I bite my lip. Discipline and routine were in plentiful supply at my old high school, but they didn't stop me from going off the rails. Will Australian discipline and routine be any different?

'There's a very good all-girls' school ten minutes from the house,' Dad is saying. 'Willowbank gets excellent exam results, and they've agreed to take you on. Why pay out a fortune for a private school with a fluffy, feel-good ethos when you can have a perfectly good education for free?'

'Right,' I say.

❀❀❀❀❀❀❀❀❀❀❀❀❀❀❀❀❀❀❀❀❀❀❀❀❀

'I didn't mention it to Charlotte because I thought she'd make a fuss,' he sighs. 'She'd assume it was all about the money, when in fact it's a question of available places . . . and a difference of opinion on the school ethos.'

'If you don't settle, we can always look again at Kember Grange,' Emma says.

'It won't come to that,' Dad insists. 'Honey's my daughter – she'll adapt, rise to the challenge. So what if she's pushed a few boundaries, broken a few rules? All teenagers do that, right? It's a lot of fuss over nothing. Honey doesn't need a specialist school. All that touchy-feely therapy stuff is for losers.'

I take a sharp breath in. Back home, my sister Summer is having therapy to help her fight an eating disorder. Does that make her a loser? I don't think so. Before we left she talked to me for ages about being brave enough to open up and let someone help.

'If I can do it, you can do it,' she'd said.

Summer is not a loser; she's the bravest girl I know. Dad hasn't even asked about her; or any of my sisters, come to that. Perhaps he thinks that talking about them might make me homesick?

20

❀❀❀❀❀❀❀❀❀❀❀❀❀❀❀❀❀❀❀❀❀❀❀

Maybe Dad is right, anyhow – maybe I don't need Kember Grange. I straighten my shoulders.

'I'll be fine,' I say carelessly. 'School's school, isn't it?'

'Exactly,' Dad says. 'That's my girl!'

< Text   ✪**Summer Tanberry**   Contact

❝ You're in trouble. Yes, even though you are on the other side of the world I am blaming YOU. Coco is so upset you've gone that she has been sitting in the oak tree playing that wretched violin pretty much non-stop since you left. I think I might have to start wearing earmuffs. All your fault. Come back! We MISS you, Honey Tanberry!
xoxo ❞

Spiderweb

3

I roll over, stretch out an arm and check my mobile. It's 3.55 a.m. Aussie time, and jet lag has me by the throat. I read Summer's text and smile; of all the good things about moving to the other side of the world, finally being out of earshot of the screeching, sawing racket of Coco's violin practice has to be near the top of the list.

My eyes are gritty with lack of sleep but every time I close them they spring wide open again against my will. I feel exhausted, yet my head is buzzing with a million thoughts, ideas, worries; I'm like a little kid who has overdosed on Coke, hyper and fractious and fizzing with trouble.

I check my mobile again. A whole two minutes has crawled by.

Back in Britain, it is late afternoon. My sisters will be

spreading homework books out across the kitchen table, drinking hot chocolate, chatting. I think of Coco, playing mournful violin in the oak tree, and suddenly there's a lump in my throat and an ache to match it.

I spoke to Mum yesterday, queuing at immigration to have my passport checked, to let her know I'd landed, but suddenly that doesn't seem like enough. I can't call now, not without waking Dad and Emma. My mobile says 4.05 a.m. Jet lag, you suck.

I slide out of bed and tiptoe to the kitchen, pouring myself an orange juice from the fridge. The house is strange, alien, silent. There is no familiar clutter, no mongrel dog lurking, ever hopeful, on the lookout for a morsel of cheese or a leftover sausage roll. I can't imagine Dad and Emma having pets.

Back in the bedroom, I pick up my iPhone and fire off a quick email to Mum. Rather than emailing Summer, Skye and Coco I copy them into Mum's message, but maybe my SpiderWeb page would be a better plan in the long run? I can post lots of pics and keep everyone up to speed on life in Sydney.

I haven't used it for ages. I log in to the page, wincing at the flirty profile picture and the photos of my fairground boyfriend and his mates. I thought Kes was special; I thought his friends were cool. Sadly, they didn't think the same about me.

Kes called just twice after Mum found out about the truanting and school expelled me. The first time was to ask if I was coming to his mate's party, which I couldn't, of course; I was grounded for life, guarded by my sisters, my stepdad, an ever-changing squad of concerned social workers. The second time was to tell me he thought we should finish, that I'd be better off without him; oh, and besides, he'd met someone new.

As for his friends, some sent the odd half-hearted text, but I could see them fading before my very eyes, like the cheap, rainbow-striped T-shirt I'd once washed on a ninety-degree cycle by mistake. Well, hey – their loss.

I take a deep breath and press Deactivate, and just like that my old SpiderWeb page is gone.

Creating a new page is like inventing a whole new me. I pick a username, SweetHoney, the name of the honeycomb truffle Paddy invented for me on my fifteenth birthday. I ate precisely half of one truffle and pretended I didn't like it, but actually it was amazing. I just didn't want Paddy to know that.

I like the name too. In a slightly ironic way.

I pick out a new profile picture, a close-up of me on the beach from earlier today. The picture is bright, smiley, wholesome, a big contrast to the flirty, in-your-face images on my old page. I fill in my details and fire off friend requests to Summer, Skye, Coco. I hesitate over the names of old classmates and ex-boyfriends, but this is a new-leaf moment and I decide on a clean break. If people from back home find me and add me, fine; otherwise I'll treat this page as a way to communicate with my sisters, nothing more and nothing less.

My old page had almost 500 followers, but where are they now? Where were they then, come to think of it? I always thought I was a popular girl, but the 'bad' kids forgot about me the minute I was no longer available for drop-of-the-hat rabble-rousing; the 'good' kids ditched me when I got expelled from school. Who knows, my wickedness could have been contagious.

A new page with no followers at all . . . at least this way I get to find out who my real friends are. The whole thing takes a while because I'm working on a smartphone, and

✿✿✿✿✿✿✿✿✿✿✿✿✿✿✿✿✿✿✿✿✿✿✿✿✿

there are some SpiderWeb features I can't access, but eventually I have a cool-looking page. I write a quick status about arriving in Sydney and add a picture of me standing on the steps of Sydney Opera House.

I open up a new page in the journal section of Spider-Web, but before I can write anything my mobile starts to ring and a picture of Tanglewood flashes up on the screen.

'Honey?' My sister Coco's voice shrills into my ear. She sounds like she could be in the next room, not on the other side of the world, and suddenly I'm grinning in the dark. 'Hang on,' I whisper, padding through the silent house. 'I'm going outside. It's the middle of the night, I don't want to wake everyone up.'

'Everyone?' Coco echoes, not missing a trick. 'Who's everyone? Who else is there?'

Outside the air is soft with the promise of another hot day, but the flagstones are cool beneath my bare feet. Above the rooftops I can see the sky flush pink.

'Nobody,' I tell Coco, then falter, unsure why I'm hiding the truth from her. It's the kind of lie that might be difficult to maintain. 'Well . . . just Dad's girlfriend, Emma.'

❀❀❀❀❀❀❀❀❀❀❀❀❀❀❀❀❀❀❀❀❀❀❀

'Emma?' Coco says. 'Wasn't that the name of his PA at his old job, when he lived with us?'

'Don't think so,' I huff. 'I don't remember.'

'I thought it was,' she muses. 'Still . . . a girlfriend. That must be a bit weird for you.'

'Nah, she's cool,' I bluff. 'I'm fine with her.'

Really, I have the knack of lying down to a fine art.

'So, tell me about Australia,' Coco rushes on. 'Is it amazing? Is it hot? Have you seen a kangaroo?'

'Not yet,' I laugh, deciding not to mention the kangaroo steak Dad polished off in the restaurant. 'And yes, it's epic. And hot. It's the middle of the night right now – well, five in the morning, anyhow – but it's still warm. I'm sitting out in the garden in my PJ shorts and vest . . .'

'Why are you even awake at five in the morning?'

'Because you rang, little sister,' I say patiently. 'And because I'm a bit jet-lagged. It takes a while to adjust to the new time zone. Are you missing me?'

'Like mad,' she says. 'Everything is just too . . . well, calm. No yelling. No door slamming. Nobody hogging the bathroom before school and using all the hot water!'

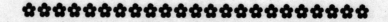

'I have my own bathroom here,' I tell her. 'And I haven't yelled or slammed a door once. I'm a reformed character.'

Coco laughs. 'Don't believe you. Not possible. You are a lost cause!'

I smile. I have vowed to put my rebel days behind me, but Coco is right, it will be hard to let go. I kind of like my old, rebel-girl self, brave and wild and dramatic.

'Are Skye and Summer there?' I ask.

'Summer's gone off somewhere with Alfie,' my little sister says. 'Skye's at Millie's, and Mum and Paddy are in the workshop. Cherry's around somewhere . . . want to speak to her?'

'What do you think?'

'That's a no then,' Coco sighs. 'Seriously, Honey, you can't hold a grudge forever.'

'Can't I? You'd be surprised . . .'

I expect my little sister to laugh, but there's just a crackly silence in my ear and suddenly I feel very tired and very far away.

'You said you were a reformed character,' Coco points out accusingly.

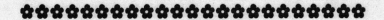

'Give me a break!' I argue. 'I'm not a saint. You can't expect me to forgive Cherry, not after what she did. Look, must we have this conversation now?'

'When will we have it then?' Coco wants to know. 'When you get home? When will that be? And . . . well, what if you never do?'

'Of course I will!' I promise. 'One day. Or maybe you'll come out here . . .'

'That won't be for years and years,' my little sister whimpers. 'You'll forget what I look like. You'll forget all kinds of stuff, miss all kinds of stuff. Families aren't meant to live thousands of miles apart!'

'Look, Coco, I didn't have a choice –'

'You had a choice,' she says, and her voice sounds muffled and wobbly. 'You just didn't choose us! I want to be happy for you, Honey, but I can't help it, I'm not. I wish you hadn't gone. It's rubbish without you!'

'Don't be like that!'

'Why not?' she sniffs. 'It's true, it is. It's like when Dad left, all over again.'

An ache of sadness lodges itself inside me. I remember how we felt when Dad went, of course I do. We were lost, hurting, wondering what we'd done wrong, what we could do to make him come back.

'This is totally different,' I say.

'It's not,' Coco chokes out. 'I miss you!'

If I could, I'd put my arms round my littlest sister and tell her everything will be fine, but hugs don't really work at long distance.

'Hey, I've just made a new SpiderWeb page and sent you a friend request,' I remember. 'We can chat on there. Tell the others, OK? Don't get all mushy on me, Coco. I'm relying on you to keep everyone in order!'

There's a snuffling sound at the end of the line, and I imagine Coco biting her lip, wiping a sleeve across her face. Unexpectedly, my own eyes prickle with tears. It's only the jet lag, of course.

'I have to go,' I say abruptly. 'Dad's calling.'

'I thought you said it was the middle of the night?' Coco argues, but I blurt out a hasty goodbye and end the call, pushing Coco's words from my head. I can't think about those things. I am in Sydney and my mum and sisters are in Somerset, and Coco's right, this is what I have chosen.

A new start, a new me.

❀❀❀❀❀❀❀❀❀❀❀❀❀❀❀❀❀❀❀❀❀

Beyond the rooftops the sky is streaked with pink as the sun begins to rise. I abandon all hope of sleep and dip a toe into the pool, experimentally. It is cold enough to make me shiver, but I don't allow myself the luxury of cowardice. I curve my body forward and dive right into the turquoise water, gasping at the shock of it.

I swim lengths until my jet-lagged brain finally switches off and my heavy heart lifts and lightens, then I roll on to my back and stretch my arms out wide, water swirling past my pale limbs as I float. The sky is brighter now, wisps of pink and gold barely visible against vivid blue.

I smile, imagining a future filled with sun and cool water, sunshades and polka-dot bikinis. Back in Britain, autumn is sliding into winter, but here in Sydney the summer is just beginning. Perhaps by flying halfway round the world, I really can turn the clock back, wipe out the mistakes of the last few months?

Notifications

Your friend requests to:
Skyeblue
Summerdaze
CoolCoco
have been accepted.

4

It's Sunday afternoon and I'm at Sunset Beach, the little surfers' cove near Dad's house. I have packed my rucksack with picnic food, iPhone, pencil case and sketchbook, and I'm hiding behind a wide-brimmed hat and sunshades.

I've had two full-on days with Dad and Emma; we've watched a modern dance production at the Opera House, driven out to the Blue Mountains and hiked along the trails, met the neighbours at an impromptu barbie and even crammed in a lightning-fast shopping trip for some truly hideous school uniform. Today Emma was seeing a friend so Dad promised me a day at the beach together, but at the last moment an important business client flew in from Singapore to talk about some big deal, and he had to drop everything.

He'll be out until late, but I don't mind. I've been itching to get out by myself, explore properly. I scope out the beach cafe, all shiny-new and open at one end with glass and decking and outside tables with sunshades. The boy behind the counter is about my age, a skinny Asian kid with blue-black hair that dips down over his eyes and a kind, crooked smile. He looks cute and friendly in a boy-next-door kind of way, but boy-next-door is not my type. I generally go for bad-boy cool, with a side order of mean 'n' moody.

I order a fresh fruit smoothie and the boy raises an eyebrow.

'You British?' he asks, chucking strawberries, banana, milk and chipped ice into a blender and hitting the button to smoosh it up.

'How can you tell?' I ask, mock-surprised. 'My English rose complexion? The tourist map peeking out of my ruck-sack? My epic fail on the whole beach dress-code issue?'

He laughs. I am probably the palest person on the beach, and the only one dressed in a flowered minidress and strappy sandals instead of a swimsuit or shorts/vest-top combo. And yes, I have a map.

'All of that,' he says. 'And the accent – dead giveaway. I like the hat and the sunglasses. Are you in disguise?'

'Might be,' I tease, tilting the hat back and peering at

❀❀❀❀❀❀❀❀❀❀❀❀❀❀❀❀❀❀❀❀❀❀❀

him over the sunglasses. On closer inspection, I can see that he has killer cheekbones and melted-chocolate eyes that take him right out of the boy-next-door category, and I smile.

'I could be a British spy,' I tell him archly. 'Or a movie star who doesn't want to be spotted, or one of those food critics who write secret reviews for the papers . . .'

'I'd better do a good job then,' he says, decanting the finished smoothie into a glass. 'Seriously – are you on holiday?'

'Not exactly – I've just moved here.'

'Cool,' he says. 'Sydney's a great place to live – I'd offer to show you around, but I'm tied up most days with school and family stuff and shifts at the cafe. Which school d'you go to?'

'I'm starting at Willowbank on Monday,' I say. 'It's all girls and pretty strict, my dad says.'

He decorates the smoothie with a slice of fresh mango and a couple of straws, sliding it across the counter while I count out my dollars and cents, trying not to look too clueless. A small queue is forming behind me.

'You'll be right,' the boy says. 'What's your name, anyhow?'

'Honey Tanberry . . .'

✿✿✿✿✿✿✿✿✿✿✿✿✿✿✿✿✿✿✿✿✿✿✿

'OK, Honey Tanberry,' he says, turning away to serve the next customer. 'I won't forget a name like that!'

I am halfway across the cafe when he shouts after me. 'My name's Ash, by the way, in case you were wondering!'

I laugh. 'I was,' I yell back. 'Obviously. Just too shy to ask!'

I'm smiling as I snag a table on the decking with a slightly wilting sunshade and set down my smoothie, spreading my drawing stuff out around me. Sunset Beach is a perfect slice of golden sand edged by a silver-blue ocean, inspiration on a plate. There are families picnicking, little kids building sandcastles, kids playing football or running into the sea.

I open my sketchbook and pick up my pencil. I love drawing people, and pretty soon I lose myself in the process. I sketch a group of girls sunbathing, smoothing suntan oil over long, tanned limbs, turning themselves like chicken on a barbecue. I draw the cute waiter with his dipping fringe and his tray of smoothies, and a middle-aged woman standing on one leg, doing yoga on the sand. A knot of teenage boys are yelling and splashing around in the ocean with surfboards, trying to catch a wave, and I draw them too, my pencil lingering over lean legs and broad shoulders, buzz-cut hair and toothy grins.

37

Suddenly, a stray football flies past, knocking my sketch-book on to the decking.

'Whoa,' a voice says, and a boy dips down to rescue the sketchbook, dusting away a scatter of sand before handing it back. 'Close one!'

He's older than me, lean and tanned and still glistening with seawater, blue eyes as vivid as the sky, damp blond hair raked back from his face. Not that I am looking, of course.

He turns and hooks the football up with one bare, tanned foot and kicks it back along the beach to where some little kids are waiting. They grab the ball and scarper, laughing.

A couple of the surfer boys are watching the whole scene play out. 'Hey, Riley!' one yells. 'Chatting up the girls again? Don't keep her all to yourself!'

'Ignore him,' the boy says. 'He's just jealous. You British?'

'Yeah . . . I've just moved here to live with my dad.'

His eyes catch mine and for a moment I think I might drown in their bright, clear blue. He likes me. He's good-looking, in an edgy, surf-boy way . . . he's like an Aussie version of my ex, Shay. And that's a good thing, trust me.

There are yells from further down the beach. Half a

38

dozen surfie boys are running towards us across the sand, all brown limbs and streaks of sunblock, surfboards beneath their arms. They skid to a halt beside us, spattering wet sand everywhere like boisterous, unruly dogs.

'Riley! C'mon, man, we've gotta bail, we'll be late. Leave the poor girl alone!'

'We're supposed to be over at Donny's for six – party time!'

'Slow down,' Riley says. 'This is . . . uh . . . I didn't catch your name!'

'Honey,' I tell him, and his eyes flash, amused.

'Honey? I like it. Sweet!'

Not so sweet, I think, remembering my ironic new Spider-Web name. But who knows, maybe a boy like Riley could halt the slow curdle of hurt inside me that turns sweet to sour? Maybe.

'Honey's new in town,' Riley is telling his mates. 'All the way from Britain! We should invite her along to the party, show her a bit of Sydney hospitality!'

'Why not?' one boy agrees. 'Pretty girls are always welcome!'

'British?' another declares. 'Cool. You doing that uni exchange scheme? Come to the party, for sure, just don't take any notice of Riley – I'm way more your type . . .'

❀❀❀❀❀❀❀❀❀❀❀❀❀❀❀❀❀❀❀❀❀❀

My heart begins a drumbeat of anticipation. This is a game I am expert at – a few cool boys, the push/pull of flirtation. There is just one problem: I am supposed to be off boys, possibly for the rest of my life. I made a deal with Dad – no boyfriends, no parties, no trouble. I am supposed to be squeaky clean. I can't break that promise on my very first week in Australia. Can I?

Dad and Emma won't be back till late. I could go to the party for a few hours and they'd never know. I'm torn, but the new-leaf me knows that this is not a good idea. 'Thanks,' I say. 'Sounds great, but . . . I can't. Sorry!'

The boys laugh and roll their eyes and pretend to be heartbroken, and then they're heading on up the beach and I'm forgotten. That's boys for you.

Deflated, I take out my iPhone and open up my new SpiderWeb page, pretending I couldn't care less. There's a post from Coco on my wall:

Hey, big sister, don't forget our Skype date tonight. I know you're starting school tomorrow and I know it is one of those crunchy granola places where you call the teachers by their first names, but . . . I want to wish you good luck. Break a leg, as Summer would say. Only . . . well, don't actually

break a leg. Obviously. Skype call is 9 p.m. your time, OK?
Your Adoring Sister,
Coco
xoxo

I'm about to tap out an answer when a shadow falls across the table: Riley.

He rakes the damp blond hair back from his face. 'Look,' he says. 'Tonight's going to be a bit crazy – don't blame you for giving it a miss. Maybe another time?'

'Maybe . . .'

His face lights up and there's a charge in the air between us, heavy but invisible. We once did an experiment about magnetism in primary school with a horseshoe magnet and iron filings, and I remember thinking it was pure magic the way one pulled the other to it. This is the same kind of magic, and I think it is working both ways.

You cannot fight that kind of thing, right? And Dad need never know . . .

'Riley!' one of his mates roars from the sand dunes. 'She's not interested in you. Come *on*!'

Riley glances at my phone. 'You're on SpiderWeb?' he asks. 'Cool. What's your SpiderWeb name?'

✿✿✿✿✿✿✿✿✿✿✿✿✿✿✿✿✿✿✿✿✿✿✿

'SweetHoney,' I say, and Riley laughs and says that figures.

Out of nowhere, Ash, the beach-cafe boy, appears at my table with a tray, collecting up my empty smoothie glass. 'OK?' he asks.

'Yeah, I'm fine!'

He wipes the tabletop down with exaggerated swipes of his cloth.

Riley rolls his eyes. 'Got a problem, mate?' he asks.

'No problem,' Ash says lightly. 'Just doing my job.'

Riley turns back to me. 'You're an art student, right?' he says. 'I live quite near to COFA, so maybe I'll see you on campus. We can grab a coffee.'

He thinks I'm older, that I'm at some kind of art college. I'm about to nod and say I'll look out for him, but even though I've just met him I feel weird blatantly lying in front of the beach-cafe boy. I've just told him I'm starting at Willowbank, after all.

'I'm not a student,' I hear myself say to Riley. 'I'm fifteen. Still at school.'

His face clouds, and the magnetism fizzles away to nothing right in front of my eyes. He's not interested in schoolkids. Why would he be?

'I'd better be getting off,' he says, sounding bored now, embarrassed. 'See you around, maybe . . .'

'Me and my big mouth,' I say to the cafe boy as he gives the table one final polish. 'Blown it.'

Ash shrugs. 'His loss,' he says.

I raise my hand to wave as Riley jogs up the beach to join his friends, but he doesn't look back.

Skye Tanberry

<skyeblue@chocolatebox.co.uk>

to me ✉

Hey, big sister, good to see you on Skype just now. We needed cheering up . . . it is very weird here without you. I came up the stairs last night, and your bedroom door was open. When I looked inside, Mum was just sitting on the window seat, hugging her knees. I think she'd been crying. I'm not telling you that to make you feel bad or anything – just that we miss you. Good luck for school and everything. Send my love to Dad . . . if he can remember who I am.

Love ya,

Skye oxox

5

The minute I walk through the doors of Willowbank School for Girls I have a bad feeling, a feeling of doom. The foyer is crowded with girls in hideous, blue-checked school uniform. They gawp at me with undisguised curiosity the way I have been gawping at parakeets in the park or surfie boys on the beach; like I am something exotic and faintly scandalous.

Don't get me wrong, I *like* being exotic and faintly scandalous. It is my trademark look, but I think I may be an endangered species here at Willowbank.

This morning when I tried on my new uniform for the first time, I almost cried.

I looked in the mirror and saw a horrified girl in a polyester tent dress with a drooping yellow neckerchief. The dress flared out into an alarming triangle shape;

knee-length white socks and ugly brown sandals completed the look. Luckily, I am an expert when it comes to adapting and improving. I used the kitchen scissors to chop three inches off the hem, hoisted it in with a belt and turned the yellow neckerchief into a hair accessory.

It wasn't good, but it was an improvement. I could tell by the way Emma's jaw dropped when she saw me.

'They're strict about uniform at Willowbank,' she argued, but I pointed out that I was wearing the uniform, every bit of it, so what was the problem?

I think I am about to find out.

The twitter of girly gossip fades into silence and I hear the clip-clop sound of high-heeled shoes approach. A woman strides towards me through the crowd, small and plump in a chiffon blouse and tailored skirt, hair fluffed and sprayed into a feathery bouffant. She peers at me over a pair of alarmingly winged glasses; she reminds me of a hen, anxious, clucking, easily ruffled.

'I am Miss Bird, the head teacher,' she tells me, and I swallow back my smirk. Miss Bird? Seriously?

'I expect you're the new girl, from England. Honey Tanberry?'

46

'Yes, Miss Bird,' I choke out.

She glares at me as if I just arrived fresh from St Trinian's with a *Danger* label tied to my wrist. I guess that's not too far from the truth, actually.

'My office,' she says. 'Now.'

A bell shrills to signal the start of class and Miss Bird ushers me into a darkly panelled room full of trophy cabinets and portraits of stern headmistresses from years gone by.

'So,' she says. 'Before we go any further – we do *not* go in for customized uniform at Willowbank. You will wear your socks pulled up to knee-length, your neckerchief round your neck. And you will let down that hem once more so it's the correct length.'

'I can't,' I say brightly, holding the jagged hemline between my thumb and forefinger. Should I go for total honesty here, or just plead ignorance? It's hard to know. Admitting that I hacked my school dress to pieces on the very first day may not be a good plan.

'There's no hem to let down,' I explain, trying for a helpless look. 'I don't know why – it just came this way. Maybe the dress was a factory reject?'

✿✿✿✿✿✿✿✿✿✿✿✿✿✿✿✿✿✿✿✿✿✿✿✿✿

'Or maybe somebody took a pair of scissors to it?' she says crisply.

'Who would *do* a thing like that?'

Miss Bird grits her teeth. 'Don't get smart with me, Honey Tanberry,' she says. 'You'll find you've bitten off more than you can chew. Let me be straight here – your father was very keen for us to take you, even at this late stage in the school year. He led me to believe that you were a bright, talented pupil with a genuine drive for success. I must say, you are not at all what I imagined.'

My eyes widen. It seems that Dad has been a little sketchy with the truth – I know I'm meant to be turning over a new leaf but I'm not sure I can live up to the saintly persona he's created for me. I take a deep breath in. I am not going to let a woman with fluffy hair and winged spectacles wreck my chances of a fresh start. I will give Willowbank a fair chance, even if it doesn't give me one . . . and I will be grateful that my murky past is finally behind me.

'Sorry, Miss Bird,' I say. 'It won't happen again. I will do my very best here, honestly I will.'

'See that you do,' she says curtly. 'Pull your socks up and take the neckerchief out of your hair. Tomorrow, I shall

48

expect perfect uniform. Your father has asked me to let him know if there is anything at all which concerns me, and believe me I will do that. Willowbank prides itself on good manners, good uniform and the desire to excel in all things, whether academic or sporting.'

'Great,' I mutter, untying my neckerchief bow.

Miss Bird sighs. 'Our coursework will be quite different from what you're used to,' she continues. 'Your father tells me he's requested the records from your old school, but they're sending paper copies of the files, so they may not reach us until the new school year. Meanwhile, I'll expect you to work hard. I want to see the determined, focused, career-driven girl your father described to me. Yes?'

'Yes, Miss Bird.'

Her eyes narrow. 'Are you wearing make-up?' she asks.

'No, Miss Bird.' Eyeliner and lipgloss don't really count, do they?

The head teacher fixes me with a beaky, speccy stare. 'I'll be watching you, Honey Tanberry,' she says. 'Remember that. Now run along – room 66, mathematics, Mr Piper.'

I dawdle along the corridor, crestfallen. Whatever happened to the creative, caring school with support for

❀❀❀❀❀❀❀❀❀❀❀❀❀❀❀❀❀❀❀❀❀❀❀

troubled students that I was promised? I might have stood a chance there. Instead I've been thrown right back into the chaos of a regular school, only with a crazed chicken-lady in charge, and minus the welcome distraction of boys. Great.

I find room 66 and take a moment outside, quickly pushing my socks down again before knocking and going inside. It's not defiance exactly – more a matter of pride.

Mr Piper directs me to an empty seat near the back. I hold my head high as my new classmates watch me slide into a seat beside a girl with black-rimmed glasses, lank auburn hair and freckles. She smiles politely, then turns back to her work.

It takes just minutes for my brain to freeze over. Maths has never been my strong point. Let's face it, my only strong points seem to be breaking the rules and messing up, and already I am top of the class in those.

'I expect you've done calculus back in England?' Mr Piper asks, pausing beside my desk. 'I don't need to explain?'

'No, no,' I bluff. 'I'll be fine.'

'Anything you don't manage today, just finish up for homework,' he says.

✿✿✿✿✿✿✿✿✿✿✿✿✿✿✿✿✿✿✿✿✿✿✿✿✿

'Right . . .' I copy out question one. It doesn't even look like a maths problem, more like a mysterious code that I don't know how to crack.

I look around the classroom. Everyone else is working, heads bent over their books, pens scratching away studiously. The girl beside me is on question five already. I don't even know where to start – I was way behind in maths back home. When my classmate Anthony offered to help me with informal after-school study sessions I jumped at the chance, but in spite of his cleverness he was never any use at explaining stuff. It wasn't long before I got bored and started sabotaging the lessons, and Anthony didn't do a thing about it. He was hooked by then. I had him wrapped round my little finger.

It ended in tears, of course. Anthony was the friend who hacked into the school computer system for me, altering my grades and sending out a fake report card. We got found out, and both of us were expelled. I am not proud of the way I treated him. I dragged him down with me, even if the hacking thing was his idea. It doesn't matter – I know he'd never have even thought of it, if it hadn't been for me.

Anyway, Anthony is history now, and if he ever tried to

❀❀❀❀❀❀❀❀❀❀❀❀❀❀❀❀❀❀❀❀❀❀❀❀

teach me calculus, I definitely wasn't listening. I begin to sketch a plump, angry chicken with a bouffant hairdo in the margin of my exercise book, and the girl beside me giggles.

'Awesome,' she whispers. 'It's Birdie, right?'

'I just thought . . . she's like this kind of bad-tempered mother hen.'

'I know!' the girl agrees. 'One crazy chook . . .'

'A tough old Bird . . .'

Mr Piper looks up abruptly, eagle-eyed, his teacher-radar on red alert. 'Is there a problem, Miss Woods?' he enquires. 'Miss Tanberry?'

'No problem, Sir,' we say together.

I go back to doodling in the margins, but this time I'm smiling.

At breaktime Tara Woods introduces me to her friend, Beneditte Jones, whose hair cascades down around her face in an avalanche of tiny braids. She has mocha-coffee skin, a curvy, cuddly shape and a riotous laugh. I like her instantly.

'Call me Bennie,' she says. 'Everybody does.'

'OK,' I say. 'So . . . does nobody around here ever break the uniform rules? Really?'

'Not much,' Tara admits. 'Lots of schools here have strict uniform rules, it's not just us. Birdie says it takes the pressure off – we get to be ourselves.'

'What if being myself involves wearing this neckerchief in my hair?' I frown, and Bennie rolls her eyes.

'Oh boy!' she says. 'I think I'm going to like you!'

'I might be a bad influence,' I tease.

'Definitely,' Tara says. 'It could get interesting!'

'Very interesting, trust me,' I say. 'Thing is, I need to stay on the straight and narrow. It's not a great time to transfer schools, and I don't want to mess up. I wasn't always a grade A student back home, but I want to do better and I have a feeling I'm going to be out of my depth. I didn't understand one single thing in maths.'

'Maths is easy,' Bennie says. 'It's just practice.'

'We can help you,' Tara offers. 'Not just with maths, but . . . well, y'know. Getting used to Sydney, used to Willowbank. If you want . . .'

I look at Tara and Bennie, two perfectly nice Australian girls who seem willing to be my friends. Thing is, they are probably *too* nice for me. They will see my true colours and ditch me fast, or else I will ruin them, bring them down to

53

my level. Tara's face is bright, innocent, believing; all those things I used to see in the mirror before I buried them deep beneath layers of bad-girl kudos. I know you can't turn back the clock, but sometimes I think I'd like to . . .

'That would be brilliant,' I say to Tara. 'Thank you.'

8 Notifications

You have new friend requests from:

Cherryblossomgirl
AlfieAnderson
LondonFinch
Millz4eva
TiaHere
BennieJ
Tarastar
Surfie16

Accept or reject?

6

I lounge beside the honeysuckle arch, my back against the flower-tangled framework, my school books scattered around me to give an impression of studying. I have four lots of homework to get through – I mean, seriously? Do Willowbank students actually have a life? Clearly not.

I've just had a quick chat on the phone to Mum, skirting round the small detail that I'm not actually at the school she thinks I am and telling her all went well. I don't think she sussed, and I told myself the lies were necessary to make sure she didn't have a go at Dad for not keeping her in the loop. My mum worries about stuff, and I do *not* want her pulling the plug on my Great Australian Adventure before it has even begun.

Emma brings me out an orange juice and tells me that

❁❁❁❁❁❁❁❁❁❁❁❁❁❁❁❁❁❁❁❁❁❁❁

dinner will be at seven – apparently, Dad is bringing home a Chinese takeaway to celebrate my first day at Willowbank.

'It's your favourite, isn't it?' she says. 'He remembered!'

'Wow . . . he really did!'

Long ago, when we were still a proper family, Dad would sometimes bring home a Chinese takeaway as a treat. He had to drive to Minehead to fetch it, so it was a really big deal, and I remember thinking that it was very sophisticated and grown-up. My little sisters weren't keen, and always ended up picking at plain white rice while Mum saved the day with a plate of hasty cheese and tomato sandwiches.

I wanted to look grown-up, so I always tried a bit of every dish, even if it meant choking down slimy beansprouts or strange vegetables dipped in hot and sour sauce. 'That's my girl,' Dad used to say, so I'd eat it all up just to please him.

When Dad left, we never ate Chinese takeaway again.

'I'm so glad it went well today,' Emma is saying. 'Look at you, getting stuck into your homework already! Greg will be proud!'

'Can you do calculus, Emma?' I ask.

She frowns. 'Can I do what?'

❀❀❀❀❀❀❀❀❀❀❀❀❀❀❀❀❀❀❀❀❀❀❀

'Never mind, I'll ask Dad later.'

As soon as Emma goes back inside, I slide a finger across the screen of my iPhone and check my new SpiderWeb page. My sisters have posted good luck messages, and there's a bunch of new friend requests from earlier.

I screw my nose up at Cherry's. I didn't send a request to her; why can't she get the message? Still, I can imagine the hassle it will cause with Skye, Summer and Coco if I refuse.

I click Accept all. Millie and Tia, friends of my sisters; Alfie, Summer's annoying boyfriend; Finch, Skye's holiday romance; Tara and Bennie from school today – that makes me smile.

Finally, I notice an add from Surfie16. I didn't have anyone on my old SpiderWeb page with that username. Maybe it's Shay? He didn't have SpiderWeb for ages, until I made a music page for him; perhaps he's made a personal page too?

I click on to Surfie16's profile page, and right away I know it's not Shay. The profile picture shows a close-up of sunbrowned feet in golden sand, part of a battered surf-board just visible in the corner; the banner is a wide, turquoise ocean with the sky streaked red and gold.

58

❀❀❀❀❀❀❀❀❀❀❀❀❀❀❀❀❀❀❀❀❀❀❀❀

My heart starts to race. These pictures were taken in Australia, surely? I think of Riley – another boy, another beach, a romance that sparked in the sunshine and fizzled just as fast to nothing.

Well, maybe I was wrong about that.

He said he'd add me on SpiderWeb, and he really has. I scan his page for clues, but Surfie16 has strict privacy settings. I can't see his friends, only a few posts on his page which range from rock-music videos shared from YouTube to short, snappy status updates about surfing. It has to be him, though!

I click on to private message.

Hey, Riley? Is this you? Great to hear from you again!
Honey xxx

Within minutes, a message appears in my inbox.

Hi, gorgeous! How's it going?

I laugh out loud. Maybe he decided that the age gap didn't matter after all – and it looks like I definitely didn't imagine the chemistry. I message again.

❀❀❀❀❀❀❀❀❀❀❀❀❀❀❀❀❀❀❀❀❀❀

Today was my first day at school in Sydney. It will take some getting used to! How was the party, anyhow?
    Honey xxx

A reply pings back almost at once.

Party was OK, but I wish you'd been there. Another time?

I grin, typing out a reply.

Maybe. And maybe I'll see you at the beach again soon?
xxx

I wait for Riley's reply, but a full ten minutes tick by before his answer arrives, by which time I'm panicking that I've scared him off. When a message finally does appear, it's short and sweet.

Sure. Got to go now, speak soon.

My shoulders slump, but hey, Riley's made contact – I can't help feeling flattered about that. I promised Dad I'd swear off boys, parties and trouble, but that doesn't mean I can't

✿✿✿✿✿✿✿✿✿✿✿✿✿✿✿✿✿✿✿✿✿✿✿

have boy *friends*, does it? A SpiderWeb friendship will hardly get me into trouble, and a little flirtation never hurt anyone. I argue myself into deciding it's OK. I am turning over a new leaf, after all, not entering a nunnery.

I turn back to my homework with a smile on my face, determined to show the teachers I can be the 'bright, talented' kid they'd been told to expect. Why not? I can be charming when I want to be, and right now it makes sense to keep the teachers onside.

Eventually, Dad arrives home with the takeaway. I have tried my very best with the homework; the science seemed straightforward enough and I ran the French translation passage through an Internet translate site. It doesn't look quite right, but hopefully it will be convincing enough. Besides, it's the best I can do right now – it's a few years since I paid any attention in French class. I still have two chapters of *Animal Farm* to read before tomorrow but hey, if jet lag strikes again tonight, at least I'll have a distraction. It's just the maths I can't get a handle on.

I tidy up my books and carry them to the house just as Dad appears in the doorway, sleeves rolled up, tie loosened.

❀❀❀❀❀❀❀❀❀❀❀❀❀❀❀❀❀❀❀❀❀❀❀

'How's it going?' he asks, flinging an arm round my shoulders. 'Lots of homework? That's what I like to see!'

'It wasn't as bad as I thought,' I say. 'I'm a bit stuck on the maths, though. Calculus. Can you explain it for me?'

'Not a problem,' he says. 'Haven't done any for a while, but I'm sure I remember the basics. Let's have a look at it after supper. This is top-quality stuff; we don't want it to go cold!'

I ditch my books on to an empty sunlounger and follow Dad across the patio. Emma puts a tablecloth and fresh flowers on the outdoor table, uncorking a bottle of wine while Dad dishes up the takeaway.

'Willowbank went well then?' he asks, handing me a laden plate. 'That's excellent. First impressions count, Honey. Be smart, be confident . . .'

'I was smart all right,' I say, remembering the way I'd cheeked Miss Bird. 'I definitely made an impression.'

Not a good one, though. A long way from good. What was I thinking?

'That's my girl,' Dad says, digging into his food.

'Miss Bird doesn't seem to know much about what

happened back home,' I venture. 'About me being expelled and all . . .'

Dad laughs. 'You think I'd broadcast that?' he says. 'There's no need for them to know the gory details. This is meant to be a fresh start, and as far as I'm concerned that means a clean sheet. You need to leave the past behind.'

'I plan to,' I say. 'But . . . Miss Bird says you've arranged for my old school records to be sent on. She won't be pleased when she finds out the truth.'

'She won't,' Dad tells me. 'I haven't spoken to your old school – that would be asking for trouble. With any luck the old bat will forget anyway, but if she asks we can just say the papers got lost in the post.'

I blink, slightly confused. This is the kind of trick I'd pull – there's no doubt at all that my rebellious streak comes from Dad. I'm not sure that a skill for lying is a great quality for a middle-aged businessman to have, but then what do I know?

Emma has switched on the music centre with its cool outdoor speakers, and the yellow light from the dining room spills out through the open patio doors. The night is warm and Dad is talking about a new account he

63

managed to nail today. Emma tops up his wine and tells him how brilliant he is – she is laying it on with a trowel, but Dad seems to like it, and from the way they're cuddling up I think it's time I made myself scarce. Seriously, you'd think older people would be past all of that mushy stuff. Shouldn't they be focusing on middle-aged pastimes like golf or gardening?

Whatever. This is clearly not the moment to mention maths homework.

I scoop up the empty foil trays and stack the plates and cutlery, carrying them into the kitchen. I rinse the foil trays and fold them flat for the recycling bin before stacking the plates in the dishwasher. I never did much around the house at home, not if I could help it, but here I need to look keen. I need to make myself useful.

The telephone rings, and I lift up the handset and click on to the call.

'Hello, can I help you?' I ask brightly.

There's a pause, and for a moment I think the call could be Mum, or one of my sisters, calling from the UK. I think I can hear a faint breath, a whisper of silence.

'Hello?' I say again, and abruptly the line goes dead. I

tap in the code to find the number, in case it really was Mum, but an automated voice tells me that the number cannot be disclosed.

'Honey, love, can you bring out the fruit salad from the fridge?' Emma calls, and I shrug off the phone call and carry out the big bowl of jewel-bright fruits.

'Somebody rang,' I say, setting everything down on the table. 'But the line went dead as soon as I spoke.'

'Probably one of those automated dial things from a call centre somewhere in who knows where,' Dad says, taking a sip of wine.

'Maybe,' Emma agrees, dishing out the fruit salad. 'Or maybe it's just some sad little creature who thinks it's OK to call up a family in the middle of their supper and then hang up.'

I blink. Emma's reaction seems a bit over the top, but who knows, perhaps she's had a hard day at work?

'Emma,' Dad says, 'it was an automated sales call. No big deal.'

'If you say so,' Emma shrugs.

I tune out their low-level bickering and think of this afternoon's messages from Surfie16 with a smile. So far, on

❀❀❀❀❀❀❀❀❀❀❀❀❀❀❀❀❀❀❀❀❀❀❀

balance, Australia is looking good. I open up *Animal Farm* and start to read, and darkness wraps itself around me, soft and warm.

Charlotte Tanberry
<charlotte@chocolatebox.co.uk>
to me ✉

Hello Honeybee . . .

    Great to talk to you earlier. I'm so glad your
first day at school was good, but still, I can't help
missing you. The big chocolate order is finished
now and Lawrie and his mum and sister are leaving
tomorrow, so we're having a farewell supper.
Guess it's night-time where you are, but I just
wanted you to know I'm thinking of you.
Love you,
Mum xxx

7

I am not sure how long jet lag is meant to last, but I'm pretty sure it should be gone by now. I have been in Sydney for ten days, but even though I fall asleep at roughly the right time each evening, I am still waking up at four in the morning, head buzzing. I think I am becoming nocturnal.

Instead of staring wall-eyed at the ceiling, I pick up my mobile and click on to SpiderWeb. Coco has posted a photo of Caramel, her new pony, on to my wall, so I hit Like and write *cute* underneath it. It is easier to be nice to my sisters when they are thousands of miles away, somehow.

A new message pops up almost at once.

Hey, big sister! Missing you. Mum says you're probably
asleep but I wish we could talk . . .
Coco

Grinning, I type out a reply.

I'm not asleep. Want to Skype?

Seconds later, a new message appears.

You betcha!

I shrug on a sweatshirt and pad through to Dad's study,
picking up his laptop and bringing it back through to my
bedroom. I am only supposed to use it for emergencies, but
talking to my sisters in the middle of the night has to qual-
ify, right? There's a familiar whoosh as the Skype icon
launches; with two more clicks the screen is filled with a
fuzzy image of the kitchen at Tanglewood, my sisters leaning in towards the camera, pulling faces.

'Can you hear me?' Coco yells, loud enough to wake the
dead. 'Can you see me?'

'I can see your left nostril really clearly,' I tell her.

❀❀❀❀❀❀❀❀❀❀❀❀❀❀❀❀❀❀❀❀❀❀❀

'Everything else is a blur, but . . . hang on . . . think you might have forgotten to wash your neck this morning, Coco!'

'The cheek!' she rages. 'A whole week, I have been pining for you! Weeping into my pillow! Playing violin laments from the treetops! You are heartless, Honey Tanberry, heartless!'

'That's why you love me,' I tease.

'Coco, move back a bit, let your sisters see the screen!' Mum's voice cuts in, and as Coco pulls back and flops down on to a kitchen chair I can finally see Mum, Skye and Summer crowding in behind her. My sisters are laughing, waving, huddled in thick jumpers next to the Aga, cradling mugs of steaming hot chocolate. For a split second I wish I was there with them, in the crowded, cosy evening kitchen at Tangle-wood and not here, alone, on the other side of the world.

'We have got *so* much to tell you!' Coco blurts.

'We miss you!' Summer adds.

'Come back, all is forgiven!' Skye says. 'Seriously! It's just not the same without you here! Are you settling in? Are you still loving it?'

'It's awesome,' I tell them. 'The sky here is so big and

so blue . . . there are parrots in the treetops and a beach just five minutes from the house! It's like paradise, honestly!'

'How's Dad?' Summer wants to know. 'Is it weird living with him?'

'No, Dad's great,' I answer. 'It's like he really belongs here, you know? It's great to spend time with him again – we've always been on the same wavelength. His business is doing brilliantly, so obviously he works hard but he's always got time for me . . .'

This is almost true, I think to myself.

'I don't suppose he's around?' Coco asks hopefully, and I shake my head.

'It's four in the morning,' I say. 'He's asleep!'

'Why aren't you?' Mum wants to know. 'You're not jet-lagged still, surely?'

'Just a little bit,' I admit. 'I'm using Dad's laptop to Skype, but I'm supposed to ask first so I really don't want to wake him up.'

'Wait there,' my littlest sister says. 'Don't go away . . . I'll be back in a minute.' She slips out of the picture abruptly, and Mum takes her place on the kitchen chair.

❀❀❀❀❀❀❀❀❀❀❀❀❀❀❀❀❀❀❀❀❀❀❀❀

'How's school?' she wants to know. 'Still good? Is it as supportive as it looked on the website?'

As before, I sidestep the question. The last few days at Willowbank have been better – I am trying hard to toe the line, but I wouldn't describe the place as supportive, exactly. I can't help wishing I'd gone to Kember Grange as planned, but Mum mustn't find out anything about that.

'You'd like Tara and Bennie,' I say, steering the conversation into safer territory, and as I say it I realize I like them too. Tara and Bennie are not the type of girls I'd have hung out with at home, but they're kind and clever and funny. Maybe, just maybe, they could be real friends, the kind of friends I've never had?

'What are your Christmas plans?' Skye is asking. 'I know it's summer in Australia, but it's Christmas too, and I don't see how that would work . . . I can't imagine it!'

'My plans for Christmas are blue skies and chill-outs at the beach,' I declare. 'Definitely not ancient tree decorations and wearing socks in bed because the central heating's on the blink!'

Mum laughs. 'You're making me jealous,' she says. 'It's

going to be very strange at Christmas without you around, but I am honestly so proud of you for making this fresh start, Honey.'

'I won't let you down,' I promise.

'I just want you to be happy,' Mum says, wiping a sneaky tear away with her sleeve, and for a fleeting moment I forget blue skies and new starts and surfer boys; suddenly I want to be home, with my mum and my sisters.

I push the thought away firmly.

'So,' I say to my sisters, 'what's your news? What am I missing?'

'Well,' Skye says, 'last week we were in Exeter and we saw a whole display of our truffles in the supermarket. They're selling really well. The Chocolate Box is going to be a famous brand!'

I pull a face. I can just imagine Paddy, swanning around like he's some kind of twenty-first-century Willie Wonka. There are advantages to being several thousand miles away from Tanglewood – I don't have to see his smug face or Cherry's sickly smile.

'Nice,' I say, a little sourly.

'I've had a letter from Jodie,' Summer tells me, changing

73

❀❀❀❀❀❀❀❀❀❀❀❀❀❀❀❀❀❀❀❀❀❀❀

the subject. 'She's almost finished her first term at the Rochelle Academy. She's loving it . . . I think she's feeling a bit guilty about taking my place, but honestly, Honey, I am almost glad things have worked out this way. It sounds so strict, so full-on.'

'You used to *like* strict and full-on,' I comment.

She laughs. 'I know . . . but look where that got me!'

I look at Summer, leaning on the back of Mum's chair, her too-thin body disguised in an outsize pink sweater, her cheekbones sharp, blue eyes shadowed. She is still beautiful, but she looks worn out, exhausted; it will take time for her to get properly well again.

'How's it going?' I ask, treading carefully, because usually we don't mention Summer's eating disorder to her face. It's as if the slightest whisper of it might cause her to break into little pieces that can never be put together again.

'Fine, fine,' she says brightly. 'I'm still going to the clinic, still working on stuff. I haven't actually put on any weight this week, but I'm not losing either . . . that's got to be good, right?'

I bite my lip, anxiety flooding through me. I was the first person to notice that Summer was getting ill a few months back; what if she gets sick again and I'm not around to help?

❀❀❀❀❀❀❀❀❀❀❀❀❀❀❀❀❀❀❀❀❀❀

Summer's twin, Skye, leans in to the camera. 'Guess what?' she says. 'That film you and Coco were in during the summer will be on TV soon. We've seen trailers for it already, with Shay's song as the soundtrack! We're going to have a big movie night with popcorn and everything!'

'Oh – I'd forgotten about that!' I say. 'We were only extras, but it was such a cool day! I'd like to see it, but I don't suppose it will be on over here.'

'It'll be on *Watch-Again*, afterwards,' Mum says. 'Ask Greg to let you watch on his laptop. You can't miss your own TV debut!'

'I won't,' I promise. 'Remember those funny Edwardian costumes we had to wear?'

'I'm going through a Victorian phase just now,' Skye tells me, leaning in to show me her new hat, a little blue velvet number with a CND badge pinned to the side. 'I found a stash of old lace petticoats in the Oxfam shop in Minehead – how cool? I'm wearing them to school and the teachers haven't said anything . . .'

'I bet you look great,' I tell her. 'Have you seen my uniform? It's a crime against humanity!'

I take the freshly washed and ironed tent dress and hideous yellow neckerchief down from their coat-hanger, holding them up against me, doing a wiggle for the webcam. Skye and Summer recoil, pretending to make themselves sick.

'But . . . I thought the school was non-uniform?' Mum asks, confused, and too late I realize I've put my foot in it big style.

'Um . . . they've had a radical change of policy,' I say, thinking quickly. 'Brought back uniform, so that everyone is . . . equal. Just my luck, huh?'

Mum frowns. 'How strange! It just seems such a turn-around for them, against their whole free expression ethos . . .'

Miraculously, Coco chooses that exact moment to elbow her way in front of the screen with her pet sheep Humbug in her arms, and Mum's words are lost in the resulting chaos. Summer lifts Fred the dog up so I can see him and even Cherry and Paddy appear, crowding in at the edges of my screen, waving.

Suddenly my bedroom door swings open and Dad stands there in his PJs, arms folded, face stern. Oops. Busted.

'I have to go,' I say abruptly. 'Look, I'll Skype again soon, promise.'

'Hang on!' Skye is saying. 'There's loads I wanted to say. You can't go yet!'

'Wait!' Coco screeches. 'I was going to bring Caramel in to say hello –'

The call disintegrates as Mum tells Coco she can't bring a pony into the kitchen, and the screen is a mess of leaping dogs and sheep and sisters, everything pixellated and blurry. I cut the call abruptly.

'Honey?' Dad says calmly. 'What's going on?'

'I was awake,' I bluster. 'Talking to my sisters on Spider-Web. And I just thought I'd Skype. I didn't think you'd mind . . .'

Dad closes the lid of his laptop firmly.

'Of course you can Skype your sisters,' he says. 'That's not an issue. But not in the middle of the night, when Emma and I have work tomorrow, and you have school.'

He shakes his head. 'You need to think before you act, consider how your actions might affect others. Your chatter woke me up, and I need to be fresh for work because I have a very busy day ahead. And you've taken my laptop without

77

permission, which really isn't on. What happened to the new start, Honey?'

I try to answer, but without warning my throat tightens and my eyes brim with tears. Letting Dad down is the last thing I wanted. I want him to see the best in me, not the worst; I want him to see how similar we are.

'Sorry,' I whisper. 'I'll try harder, I promise.'

Dad sighs. 'Look, you know how I feel about this now,' he says. 'Let's leave it at that, start over. I can see that you need to talk to your sisters now and then . . . and I imagine a laptop might be useful for schoolwork too. I expect you could do with one of your own.'

I blink. Is Dad offering to buy me my own laptop?

'C'mon, Princess,' he says gruffly, putting an arm round my shoulders. 'No more tears – you're a tough cookie. Now, let's both grab some sleep before those darned alarms go off, right?'

'R-right,' I agree.

I dredge up a wobbly smile.

Seriously, even when he's angry, my dad is pretty awesome.

Coco Tanberry
<coolcoco@chocolatebox.co.uk>
to me ✉

It was fab to Skype last night. Things at Tanglewood are way calmer now that Lawrie and his family have gone, but I do miss them, Lawrie especially. Not in a mushy way – it's just that we went through so much with the ponies and even though I thought he was annoying to start with, we ended up being best friends. Have you ever had a best friend who was a boy, Honey? I tried to tell Jayde and Sarah and Amy about it and they said you can't have a boy as 'just' a friend, but I think that's rubbish.

Anyway, the best thing of all is that they left Caramel. Lawrie's mum said she couldn't think of anyone better to look after her and Mum and Paddy agreed, so I FINALLY have my own pony. Sort of. How cool is that? When I'm with Caramel, everything seems better, though I still miss you loads, obviously. And Lawrie, just a bit.

Your FAVOURITE sister,

Coco xoxo

8

Dad was right about one thing. I am a tough cookie; my new life in Australia is going to be awesome.

Things at Willowbank are a bit better; I am wearing my socks pulled up, my collar on the outside, my tent dress neatly hemmed and the yellow neckerchief tied jauntily round my neck. Every day I fix a winning smile on my face and set out to wow the staff and students, and it works, a little bit. I begin to relax, fit in. For the first time in years I am trying to make a good impression instead of a bad one.

My teachers soon suss that I am not the teen genius Dad made out and offer me study notes and extra homework to help me catch up with missed coursework. I smile and pretend to be grateful, and in spite of a strong urge to throw the extra work into the nearest bin, I take it home and do the best I can. What can I say? It passes the time in the middle of the night when jet lag comes to call.

Art is the only subject I am actually good at – when Miss Kelly flicks through my sketchbook, her face lights up.

'So much potential,' she says, and I bite my lip and hold my head high because it is so long since I've had a compliment from a teacher I don't quite know how to react. I have potential. Who knew?

It's not all fun and games, obviously. On Friday, I stay on for Mr Piper's after-school maths study group, so that he can get a better idea of the gaping holes in my mathematical education and work out where to start patching them up. In the past, staying after school usually meant detention. Staying because I've chosen to feels deeply weird, but Tara and Bennie go to study group too; it's a group for people who love maths as well as those who struggle.

'You'll like it,' Tara says. 'Maths is cool!'

I smile weakly. Me and a dozen geek-chic girls . . . life is clearly having a laugh at my expense.

I fix on my winning smile and try very hard to listen to Mr Piper, even though my brain feels like it will freeze over any moment. Luckily, he has the patience of a saint, which is just as well. My progress is painfully slow. But progress is progress, and my reward is looming.

This morning, over breakfast, Dad arranged to pick me up after study group so that he can take me to buy a laptop. He says it is an early Christmas present, but that it makes sense to buy it now; it will focus my mind and help me with my studies, and by the time the holidays start I will be well on the way to catching up with my coursework. That and the fact that I won't be creeping about the house at four in the morning to Skype home on his work laptop, of course.

'Are you catching the bus, or shall we walk?' Bennie wants to know as we emerge into the sunshine after school. 'We could call into the cafe at Sunset Beach and grab some Cokes to celebrate the weekend!'

'I can't,' I tell her. 'Dad's picking me up. We're going laptop shopping!'

'Wow!' Tara exclaims. 'Really? That's so cool! Your dad sounds amazing!'

'He is pretty awesome,' I agree. 'There was no chance of having a laptop of my own when I lived with Mum . . .

❀❀❀❀❀❀❀❀❀❀❀❀❀❀❀❀❀❀❀❀❀❀❀❀

we just didn't have the cash. But Dad says it's an essential, if I am serious about my studies. He's really generous!'

Just then, my mobile buzzes.

> Honey, not going to make it today after all – I have a last-minute meeting that looks set to run late. I'll sort something tomorrow, OK? x
>   PS: Tell Emma not to wait for me for supper. I'll grab a sandwich at my desk. x

My shoulders slump. Dad has let me down before, of course, but I hoped things would be different here. Still, I guess he can't help it if an important meeting comes up.

'Problem?' Bennie asks.

'Yeah . . . Dad can't make it,' I say. 'Some big meeting. Which means just one thing, obviously . . .'

'What?'

'I'm all yours,' I announce, hooking my arms through Tara and Bennie's and setting off along the road. 'Let's hit the beach!'

I don't really expect to see Riley at the beach, but I can't help scanning around just in case. He's not there, of

❀❀❀❀❀❀❀❀❀❀❀❀❀❀❀❀❀❀❀❀❀❀❀

course. Some kids are playing cricket and a few people are walking dogs, but it's much quieter than Sunday. 'I was going to suggest we do something tomorrow,' Bennie says as we lie on the sand. 'Go into town, go shopping or something . . .'

I shrug. 'Sounds good. I need to find some Christmas presents for my mum and sisters. I have to post them soon if they're to arrive in time.'

'OK,' Tara says. 'Great! We should have a sleepover soon too. Eat pizza and watch movies and paint each other's nails!'

This sounds like something my little sister Coco would do with her friends, but I smile politely and pretend to be thrilled. I am out of practice at having friends; some time over the last couple of years, my middle-school mates dropped by the wayside, scared off by my wild ways; the hard-faced girls I replaced them with were never really friends, I can see that now. With Tara and Bennie, I am starting right back at the beginning.

'We could do makeovers,' I say carefully, eyeing the girls speculatively. 'Try some different styles ready to wow the boys at all those Aussie Christmas parties!'

'I don't think I'm going to any Christmas parties,' Tara laments. 'Only small, family ones, with grannies and bearded great-uncles who smell of cough sweets.'

'Wowing the boys is not easy for us,' Bennie says. 'That's where going to an all-girls' school sucks. We've no idea how to act. We can't flirt, we can't slow-dance . . . we're clueless!'

'We are,' Tara confirms. 'Two weeks ago, I was waiting at the bus stop when a lad from the boys' school asked me if I had a pen he could borrow. I got so flustered I couldn't actually speak – I went crimson, shoved a biro into his hand and ran away.'

'She really did,' Bennie confirms. 'Faster than the hundred-metre dash on Sports Day!'

'If a boy tried to kiss me, I'd faint with terror,' Tara adds. 'I am a lost cause.'

My eyes widen. 'Hang on,' I check. 'You've never kissed a boy? Really?'

Tara shrugs her shoulders, a slow burn of pink staining her cheeks. 'OK, so I'm a slow learner. Strict parents, all-girls' school. I've just never met the right boy. Or any boy, come to think of it. I've led a sheltered life.'

85

'You're not missing much,' Bennie says cheerfully. 'I kissed a boy called Bernard Harper on holiday on the Gold Coast last year, and it was a bit like eating lukewarm soup without a spoon. All slobbery and awkward.'

'You never told me that!' Tara gasps.

'It wasn't even good soup,' Bennie says thoughtfully. 'More like dishwater. Boys are overrated. He asked me out and I said it'd never work because we lived so far apart, but really it was all about the dishwater kisses.'

'Not all boys are dishwater,' I tell Tara and Bennie. 'I've known a few who were pure melted chocolate. They're the ones that make it all worthwhile.'

I think of Shay Fletcher, who was definitely chocolate. There've been others since, and I thought that they were chocolate too, at the time; most turned to dishwater in the end, like Kes.

Tara sighs. 'Wow! Have you kissed many boys, Honey?'

I laugh. 'Too many. Bennie is right – there are plenty of dishwater lads out there. It's better to wait for that first kiss, make sure it's special.'

'But how will we meet cool boys when we're at an all-girls' school?' Tara wails.

❀❀❀❀❀❀❀❀❀❀❀❀❀❀❀❀❀❀❀❀❀❀❀❀

'Easy,' I say. 'They're everywhere! I bet I can find you some lads once the holidays start – the chocolate kind. Meanwhile, I'll train you up in the art of flirting. And we may as well start now . . .'

Bennie looks around the beach, frowning. An eight-year-old with a cricket bat and a middle-aged man in polka-dot board shorts are the only eligible males in sight, but if I narrow my eyes and squint into the shady reaches of the beach cafe, I can just about see Ash, the cute waiter with the table-cleaning obsession. He might do for flirting practice for Tara and Bennie.

'Chill,' I tell my friends. 'The first lesson is to ditch the anxiety – boys are not an alien species. Well, actually, they kind of are, but that's OK! You need to understand that you are gorgeous, clever, confident . . .'

'Not me,' Tara says. 'Any boy comes within a five-kilometre radius and I'm a nervous wreck.'

'Not any more,' I say. 'Last one to the ocean buys drinks all round! Come on!'

I grab their hands, the way I used to years ago with my little sisters, dragging them out across the sand. We hurtle forward, schoolbags flapping, the three of us screeching, laughing, howling. The day's rules and regulations peel away and I stop caring about whether I am a rebel, a rule-breaker, a no-hope girl . . . or a newly invented version of myself, someone with potential. None of that matters.

I reach the water's edge first, throwing down my bag, kicking off my shoes and socks. The next moment I am in the water, shrieking, splashing, kicking up long plumes of surf. It feels childish, exhilarating. 'Now,' I announce, knee-deep in the surf. 'The important bit. When I was little, my sisters and I used to make wishes at the water's edge, and they almost always came true. We're going to make a wish too. For sunshine, for friendship, for cool boys and true love . . .'

I take their hands in mine again, as if we are all five years old, pushing down towards the water.

'Hope it works,' Tara says. 'I'm wishing for that first kiss . . .'

Bennie laughs. 'I'm wishing for a chocolate boy.'

I scrunch my eyes closed and one thought flashes across my mind as my hands, twined with Tara and Bennie's, dip into the ocean. *I just want to be happy . . .*

A huge, icy wave breaks over us and we pull apart, screeching, clamouring for the shore. My face is sore from laughing so hard and my lips taste of saltwater.

'Honey Tanberry,' Bennie gasps, twirling round on the sand, 'you are officially crazy! I haven't laughed so much for ages!'

'I am soaked,' Tara groans. 'I think I swallowed half the bay!'

'You were the last in the water, Tara,' I point out, grinning. 'You get the drinks. That was the deal!'

'No way!' she argues. 'I'm not going into the cafe looking like this!'

I look at Bennie. 'Don't even ask,' she protests. 'Look at us, Honey! We're like drowned rats!'

'Oh, for goodness' sake! Watch and learn . . .'

I shake my hair and smooth down my dress, the hem still dripping, and stride across the hot sand to the cafe, my schoolbag swinging. Tara and Bennie follow, grabbing up stray shoes and socks, giggling.

The beach cafe is deserted except for Ash, sitting on a bar stool reading a book. He looks up as I walk in, scanning my damp hair, my bare feet, the dark, wet patches on my

✿✿✿✿✿✿✿✿✿✿✿✿✿✿✿✿✿✿✿✿✿✿✿

dress. Tara and Bennie stumble to a halt behind me, pink-cheeked and dripping.

'Honey Tanberry,' he says, and I am secretly pleased that he remembers my name.

He raises an eyebrow. 'Been swimming?'

'It's a hot day,' I quip. 'Couldn't resist.'

'It might be different in Britain, but I have to tell you, most people here get changed first . . .'

'We are not most people,' I tell him. 'We like to be different. These are my school friends, Tara and Bennie. Girls, this is Ash.'

'Good to meet you,' he says.

'Hello,' Bennie gabbles. 'We weren't actually swimming – it was just paddling really, and then we got soaked by this huge wave that came out of nowhere . . .'

'I saw,' Ash says. 'Looked like fun!'

'It was!' Bennie agrees. I notice she is holding Tara firmly by the arm, as if she might wriggle free and make a run for it any minute.

'You were going to order something, Tara,' I remind her. 'Right?'

'Mnnnnfff,' Tara says through gritted teeth, her

✿✿✿✿✿✿✿✿✿✿✿✿✿✿✿✿✿✿✿✿✿✿✿✿

face scarlet. 'I mean . . . um . . . three Cokes, please.'

Ash slides down from the bar stool and heads behind the counter, and I pick up the abandoned book, a dog-eared philosophy text. It's a pity Ash has major geek-boy tendencies because he's very good-looking, in a dark and smouldering kind of way.

'Are you at uni?' Bennie asks.

'School,' he says. 'Got my Higher School Cert next year.'

'Oh . . . Nietzsche,' Tara says, picking up the book. 'I'm quite interested in philosophy . . . I thought I might want to do it at uni.'

'Yeah?' Ash asks, pouring Coke into chilled glasses. 'I have a couple of books you can try. Schopenhauer and Descartes, but fairly basic . . .'

Tara's boy phobia seems to have vanished – she and Ash are chatting happily about weird, long-dead boffins. It's a little disconcerting.

'Whatever,' I say, rolling my eyes. 'My philosophy is simple – live for the moment and make every second count. And have as much fun as you can, obviously.'

'That's definitely the impression I'm getting,' Ash says, his attention back on me. 'So . . . ice-cream floats in the

❀❀❀❀❀❀❀❀❀❀❀❀❀❀❀❀❀❀❀❀❀❀❀❀

Cokes then? On the house. One-time special offer for mermaids only?'

'We're not mermaids!' Bennie giggles.

'But we'll take the free drinks,' I cut in. 'Thanks!'

Tara and Bennie take their drinks and head outside into the sunshine. As I turn to follow, Ash touches my arm and I shiver a little.

'You're quite something, Honey Tanberry,' he says. For about a millisecond I think that's a compliment, and then I remember the wet hair hanging around my face in rat's-tail ringlets, the sea-splashed school dress, the shallow puddle forming around my sand-crusted feet. If it *is* a compliment, it is the strangest one ever.

I start to laugh, and Ash laughs too, and it feels like the start of a friendship.

I don't get home until after six. I forgot to call Emma to pass on Dad's message, and she's cooking something complicated and stressful involving several recipe books and most of the contents of the kitchen cupboards. Everything is strewn across the kitchen as if a small tornado has just passed through, and she looks a little overwhelmed.

❀❀❀❀❀❀❀❀❀❀❀❀❀❀❀❀❀❀❀❀❀❀

'Did you get your laptop?' she asks, tucking a strand of hair behind one gold-hooped ear. 'Is it nice? Where's Greg?'

'Change of plan,' I explain. 'Dad texted – he'll sort the laptop at the weekend because something came up at work. He won't be home for dinner . . . said he'd get a sandwich at his desk.'

Emma's face falls. 'But . . . I've gone to all this trouble,' she says helplessly.

I bite my lip. 'I was supposed to tell you, but I went to the beach with Tara and Bennie. I didn't know you were making something special. I'm sorry!'

'It's not your fault,' Emma says. 'He should have called me himself. He promised he'd make an effort, spend more time at home.'

I jump to defend Dad. 'It was an emergency,' I assure Emma. 'He'd never have let us down if he could help it. He works so hard!'

'Too hard sometimes,' Emma sighs, but then she wipes the frown from her face and fixes on a smile. 'You're right, Honey, it's a high-pressure job with a lot of responsibilities. It does mean late nights sometimes. Greg works hard so we get to enjoy a certain kind of lifestyle – a house with a

❀❀❀❀❀❀❀❀❀❀❀❀❀❀❀❀❀❀❀❀❀❀

pool, luxury holidays, meals out; of course, he has to support you and your sisters too . . .'

It's my turn to frown. Before Paddy was on the scene I remember times when we were scarily short of cash, and even now, it's not like we could afford half the mod cons in this place.

'Oh, well – we'll make the best of it. Let's have a girls' night in!' Emma says.

We watch a DVD called *10 Things I Hate About You*, a teen movie from Emma's youth that is actually quite cute, curled up on the sofa, eating as we watch. The meat is charred on the outside and raw on the inside, and the carefully prepared sauce cold and lumpy, but neither of us comment, and the pudding, ice cream with chocolate sauce, is much better. We watch the screen and laugh and say 'awww' at the slushy bits.

'Bring your new friends over any time,' Emma says. 'This is your home too – you could have a sleepover or a pool party or a movie night.' She looks childishly excited at the idea, and it strikes me that for all her gorgeous house and privileged lifestyle, she is actually a little lonely.

When the film is over I help to wash up and tidy the kitchen, then head to my room. When I go to check SpiderWeb, to my surprise there's a message from Surfie16, posted just a few minutes ago.

> Hey, gorgeous . . . just wanted you to know you're on my mind.

I grin and a moment later another message flashes up.

> So, how's school? Bet you're popular with the boys!

I laugh then type.

> It's an all-girls' school. Besides, I don't have time for boys . . . I'm way too busy with my studies. I am a model pupil! xxx

A reply pops up almost at once.

> Yeah, that'll be right! I bet they don't know what's hit them!

I frown. I was on my best behaviour that day at the beach, so why is it so hard for Riley to believe I could be a model pupil? Sometimes I think I may as well have *bad girl* tattooed

❀❀❀❀❀❀❀❀❀❀❀❀❀❀❀❀❀❀❀❀❀❀❀

across my forehead because no matter how hard I try, people label me that way. It's kind of depressing. I type, a little huffily.

It's true. I'm fitting in just fine.

There's a pause, and then an answer appears.

Just teasing, OK? Gotta go, but we'll talk again. I'm always here.

I click away from SpiderWeb, relieved that Riley didn't mean anything by the comment – the fact is, he's out there, and he's thinking of me. I open up a school book and try to focus on homework, but my mind keeps drifting back to last Sunday at the beach. What if I'd said yes to Riley's invitation? Would that have been so very bad?

It's late when I hear Dad come in. My homework is long finished and I'm curled up in bed in the dark, balanced on the edge of sleep. I hear Emma's voice, a rising howl of anguish. 'Can't you at least tell me when you're going to be this late? It's past midnight, Greg. It's not fair, you know it's not!'

❀❀❀❀❀❀❀❀❀❀❀❀❀❀❀❀❀❀❀❀❀❀❀❀

'It was unavoidable, sweetheart,' Dad says soothingly.
'Shhh, now. We don't want to wake Honey.'

I let go, sliding helplessly into a world of dreams.

Skye Tanberry
<skyeblue@chocolatebox.co.uk>
to me ✉

Just to let you know we are wrapping up your
Christmas prezzies today. Expect a box of
goodies soon! And no peeking till Christmas!
Only 22 sleeps to go!
Skye
xxx

9

I lie awake at four in the morning and stare at my bedroom ceiling. There is nothing much to look at; just plain white plaster, shadowy in the lamplight. At Tanglewood, my ceiling was a faded sky blue, collaged with little gold stars made out of sweet wrappers. The year I was nine, Mum spent a week painting the ceiling while I made the stars, folding, cutting, glueing. We stood on ladders to stick them up there and the end result was beautiful, a child's picture of the sky, infinite blue.

'If you ever feel fed up, you can wish on them,' she'd said.

I don't believe that sweet-wrapper stars can chase away your troubles, of course, but I found them comforting. I wished on those stars the year Dad left, and again when

❀❀❀❀❀❀❀❀❀❀❀❀❀❀❀❀❀❀❀❀❀❀❀❀

Shay ditched me for my stepsister. They didn't work, clearly, but still.

My mobile says it's 04.03 on Friday 8 December, and I am wide awake. Again.

I don't know if I can call it jet lag any more, not almost three weeks in, but who cares? Jet lag, insomnia, it all adds up to the same thing. At least for the last few days I've had more to distract me than maths homework and French translations.

The middle of the night is when I talk to Riley.

When I can't face another equation and the sky outside my window is still ink-black, I click on to SpiderWeb and, almost always, Riley is there. I think he is nocturnal too. Sometimes he's just home from a party, sometimes he's been up all night writing a last-minute essay, another time he'd woken early to go for a run along the beach. Not Sunset Beach, sadly. He lives way out on the other side of Sydney, which is why I haven't bumped into him again.

A SpiderWeb romance has its limitations, though, and I'm the kind of girl who likes to keep her options open. If

❀❀❀❀❀❀❀❀❀❀❀❀❀❀❀❀❀❀❀❀❀❀❀

my early mornings are all about flirting with Riley, my afternoons are about chilling with Ash. I have taken to calling in at the beach cafe on my way home from school, and most afternoons he is there, reading or studying or serving customers. I buy a smoothie and sit up on one of the tall bar stools at the counter, and we talk and work and flirt a little.

So yeah . . . life in Sydney is cool. I went shopping on Saturday with Tara and Bennie, admired the giant Christmas tree in Chiffley Plaza, the trees hung with fairy lights, the department stores piping Christmas carols into cool, air-conditioned interiors when outside the heat was stifling. It was weird to be Christmas shopping in shorts and a T-shirt, but I picked out the perfect presents for Mum, Skye, Summer and Coco. I even bought nail varnish in an especially nasty shade of mustard for Cherry and a packet of TimTam chocolate biscuits for Paddy, and the whole lot was wrapped and posted off days ago. I imagine that parcel, making its way round the world to Tanglewood.

School is no picnic, of course. I have years of skiving to

✿✿✿✿✿✿✿✿✿✿✿✿✿✿✿✿✿✿✿✿✿✿✿✿

make up for, but at least now I have a shiny new laptop to help with the task. Dad brought it home last Saturday to make up for the mix-up and him having to work late.

Tonight it is especially hard to make myself finish the maths study sheet I'm working on. Every question seems harder than the last, and although I keep plodding on, going through the steps Mr Piper showed me, I'm not sure my fragile pre-dawn brain can handle it all. Staying power is not a concept I have ever applied to schoolwork before, and by the time I finish, I feel like I've scaled the Blue Mountains in a pair of flip-flops and planted a flag of pride on the summit. What's on the flag? A new leaf, obviously.

I put the maths folder away, open up the laptop and click on to SpiderWeb. Sure enough, a message from Riley is waiting.

You awake, beautiful?

My lips twitch into a smile and I type back.

Don't you ever sleep? You party so hard it's a miracle you

❀❀❀❀❀❀❀❀❀❀❀❀❀❀❀❀❀❀

ever make it into uni. What did you say you were
studying again?
xxx

An answer bounces back almost at once.

Wouldn't you like to know? I take classes in surfing,
drinking and sleeping till midday, but messaging beautiful
girls in the middle of the night is my speciality.

I'm still grinning at that when the next message comes
through.

So . . . how is my favourite insomniac today?

I tap out a reply.

I'm good, how about you? Did you just get in?
xxx

I click Send, and a minute later Riley's answer appears.

What can I say? Maybe I've started to set my alarm to
5 a.m. to chat online to my favourite English girl. Or
maybe I'm a no-good party animal, destined to haunt

the after-dark, cider-stained backyards of the Sydney suburbs, searching for true love night after night and finding nothing but heartache.

My fingers fly over the keyboard.

> I think I can guess which. So . . . good party? Meet anyone cool?
> xxx

A reply appears.

> Several dozen meat-headed bozo surf kids, a handful of clueless students, three girls who looked like extras from a Frankenstein movie and one scrounging mongrel who ran off with my burger. I'm not lucky in love.

That makes me laugh out loud. I type back.

> I know the feeling. I have a knack of picking the worst boys ever. At least, I did . . . I have turned over a new leaf.
> xxx

Riley's reply appears.

❀❀❀❀❀❀❀❀❀❀❀❀❀❀❀❀❀❀❀❀❀❀❀❀❀

Snap. Only with girls, obviously. Hey, let's liven this up.
Truth or dare?

I shake my head. There's no way I am going to pick
dare – I can just imagine Riley daring me to skinny dip in
Dad's pool or cycle along the street in my PJs singing Christmas carols. Not happening. I type a reply.

Truth. Maybe!

A minute later, my challenge arrives.

So, tell me about the boys you've dated in the past. The
good, the bad, the ugly . . .

I bite my lip. This is not my idea of fun, but Riley is not to
know that.

Do I have to? Like I said, I've turned over a new leaf. I'm
off boys.

A reply appears almost at once.

Even me?

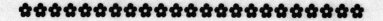

I type back.

You're different. You're one of the good guys, right?

Even as I type, I'm not sure if that's what Riley is. When I met him on the beach, he seemed like a surfer-boy version of Shay Fletcher, wholesome and sporty and cool. His messages are different, though, giving an impression of a hard-partying bad-boy.

He answers quickly.

You wouldn't be interested if I was one of the good guys, admit it. Either way, here is my past history, so you know you're not alone. The good: a girl from my old high school who had my heart for years, but didn't even notice I was alive. The bad: too many to name. The ugly: see above. And then there's you. Hoping you might fit into the 'good' category . . . a guy can dream! OK, your turn now!

I blink. No wonder I can't pigeon-hole Riley; he is a mixture of good and bad, exactly like me. Maybe we both just need the right person to break the old patterns and be the best we can be? I start to type; I'm not sure my message is the

❀❀❀❀❀❀❀❀❀❀❀❀❀❀❀❀❀❀❀❀❀❀❀❀

whole truth, but there's enough there to let Riley know I've had a messed-up past. He likes trouble too, I am pretty sure of that.

The good: a boy I dated back when I was thirteen or fourteen. He ditched me for my stepsister, so I'm guessing he didn't feel the same way. The bad: hmmm, it's a long list. Teen biker, Year 11 heart-throb, farmer's son, film student, tattooed fairground boy . . . just a few of the edited highlights. The ugly: I don't do ugly, unless you count the lovesick nobody who got me chucked out of school a while back, and . . . I don't. So yeah . . . there's a vacancy in the 'good' category right now if you want to apply? Just sayin'.
xxx

I wait for a response, but the minutes slide by and the fizz inside me goes flat, like Coke left out in the sun. I was trying to pick up on Riley's flirty, teasing tone but it's harder to get the pitch right in an online message than it is in real life. Have I said too much? The silence leaves me confused and embarrassed.

I add another line quickly.

Joking. We're just friends, right?

An answer comes back almost at once.

> Friends? You kidding me? I do not set my alarm to five in the morning to talk to my friends. Just sayin'.

Relief washes over me as I type back.

> Hey. There was me thinking you were playing hard to get . . .
> xxx

I wait for a reply, but nothing arrives.

I smile, imagining Riley stretched out on his student bunk, still in his party clothes, drifting into sleep as the Sydney dawn drags its finger along the windowpanes. I imagine his laptop glowing bright in the half-light until, finally, it blinks and sleeps too.

**Message:
Skyeblue**

Just so's you don't forget . . . your big movie debut is almost here! *Scarlet Ribbons* is on TV here at 8 p.m. on Wednesday. You should be able to get it on *Watch-Again* from the day after. So excited! Finch says you're in loads of the fairground scenes!
Skye xoxo

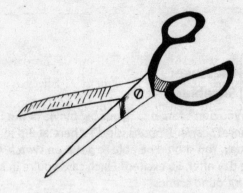

10

At Tara's sleepover, sometime after eating the home-made funny-face pizzas and watching the first slushy DVD, talk turns to makeovers. We sort through Tara's wardrobe, discarding the worst atrocities and updating others. Tara hands me a pair of dressmaking shears and I set to work turning jeans into shorts, a knee-length skirt into a mini, a T-shirt into a crop top.

'Your mum will kill me,' I say, snipping the lace collar from a prissy little print dress and holding it against a plain black T-shirt. 'But you're going to look amazing, I promise!'

'How d'you know what to do with all this stuff?' she asks. 'You should be a fashion designer or a stylist or something . . .'

'No, my sister Skye's the stylist – she loves vintage and

she can make something beautiful out of almost anything. A charity-shop dress, an old sheet . . . She's awesome, I kid you not. She helped with the costumes for a film a little while ago, and it's going to be on TV in the UK on Wednesday night!'

'A film?' Bennie echoes. 'Cool!'

I shrug. 'Me and my little sister Coco are in it as extras,' I say. 'Just in the background.'

'Serious?' Tara gasps. 'You're in a *film*?'

'I guess I am,' I say. 'It's on *Watch-Again* from Thursday. I might have a look . . .'

'You have to!' Bennie tells me. 'We will too. I can't believe you never mentioned it before!'

'It's no big deal,' I say, watching Tara lean in towards the mirror, pulling her hair back into a ponytail. She frowns, rolling her eyes.

'Hey, film star, any advice on what I can do with my hair?' she asks. 'It's just so . . . yuk. And I can never figure out what suits me.'

I narrow my eyes. Tara's hair is a startling shade of auburn, but it's too long and too lank, held back with little-girl hairslides decorated with polka dots.

❁❁❁❁❁❁❁❁❁❁❁❁❁❁❁❁❁❁❁❁❁❁❁

'Have you tried an updo?' I ask, and I open my laptop and find a YouTube tutorial. Bennie and I set to work with hairspray and backcombing to create a towering beehive-style bun, but the end result is ridiculous, as if Tara is balancing a small cushion on her head. We try French plaits next, but that looks too severe. I demonstrate making ring-letty waves with a hair straightener, but this just makes Tara look like a lovable spaniel with extra-cute ears.

'I think it's too long,' I declare finally. 'It's nice enough, but it doesn't flatter your face – you have great bone structure, Tara. What would really, really suit you is one of those short, sharp bobs, like Amélie from that French film, only . . . well, you know. Auburn.'

Tara folds her hair up short to make a mock-bob, and her face lights up. 'Maybe!' she says. 'With a cute little fringe? I've always wanted something like that, but every time I go to the hairdresser I get cold feet and ask for a trim instead.'

'Hairdressers are overrated,' I say rashly. 'Anyone can cut hair.'

Tara and Bennie turn to look at me. 'You think?' Bennie asks.

❁❁❁❁❁❁❁❁❁❁❁❁❁❁❁❁❁❁❁❁❁❁❁

'Sure,' I say confidently. 'I cut my own hair. How hard can it be?'

'That settles it,' Tara says. 'Because your hair is gorgeous!'

She hands me the dressmaking shears and I try not to panic. I did cut my own hair, sure, but only because I was really mad after that whole Cherry and Shay nightmare, and decided to hack off my waist-length blonde waves in favour of a skinhead crop. It was more self-harm than high fashion, and it took ages to grow out again. My hair is shoulder length now, but yeah, scissors and me can be a very dangerous combination.

'Are you sure?' I ask.

'Certain!' Tara insists. 'Chop it all off!'

I start very carefully, trimming one side to chin length and working my way round while she holds perfectly still. Slivers of auburn hair drop to the floor as I snip. When I get all the way round, I discover I've cut the hair shorter on that side than where I started, so I have to go back again, combing and frowning and pretending it is all part of the plan. Eventually, everything is the same length, but then Tara reminds me about the fringe.

'Fringes are hard,' I say. 'But I've seen this trick where

you stick a piece of Sellotape across the hair and cut along that. Can't go wrong.'

I comb Tara's newly short hair down across her face, administer a strip of Sellotape, then start to chop. 'See?' I declare, admiring the neat edge I've created. 'Foolproof!'

Bennie tears the Sellotape away, which makes Tara yell, and as if by magic her fringe readjusts so that it's all jagged and uneven.

'It's probably my fault,' Tara says. 'My hair has a mind of its own . . .'

By the time I have the fringe straight, it has shrunk back to just a few centimetres long, giving Tara a permanently startled appearance. Her new-look bob is dramatic all right, but miraculously, it seems to suit her. She twirls and pouts in front of the mirror and finally adds the little-girl hair-slides again, and they actually look good this time.

'Wow,' she sighs. 'I look much more grown-up and intel-lectual. Maybe boys will notice me now. Ash, maybe?'

'I doubt it,' Bennie cuts in. 'He fancies Honey.'

I raise an eyebrow. 'I don't fancy him,' I argue. 'At least . . . only a little bit. He's very cute, but not really my type.'

'What is your type?' Bennie demands.

❀❀❀❀❀❀❀❀❀❀❀❀❀❀❀❀❀❀❀❀❀❀❀

I shrug. 'I like bad boys . . . boys with a bit of edge, a bit of danger about them. The thing is, Tara, I don't think you fancy Ash either. Think about it. Did your heart beat faster when you spoke to him? Did you blush or stammer or feel awkward?'

'No,' she admits. 'But it was nice to find someone who's actually heard of Nietzsche!'

'Who?' I tease. 'But anyway, that's not the point. Fact is, there was no spark! Remember you told me about the boy at the bus stop who asked you for a pencil?'

'I went crimson,' she remembers. 'I couldn't breathe, couldn't speak. It was awful!'

'That's because you fancied him,' I explain. 'There was a spark – chemistry, if you like. That's good! It means you've hit on a chocolate boy. Once you learn to control all that and get talking, you'll be fine! What was his name?'

'Joshua McGee,' Bennie chips in. 'He lives on the corner of my street.'

'I can't talk to him,' Tara wails. 'It's impossible! I'll just make a fool of myself!'

'You won't,' I promise. 'You can control the panic – we'll work on it. Wait till he sees your new haircut!'

❀❀❀❀❀❀❀❀❀❀❀❀❀❀❀❀❀❀❀❀❀❀❀

Bennie grins, wrapping herself in a corner of duvet. 'You are all kinds of awesome, Honey Tanberry,' she says. 'I bet we'll find ourselves some cool boys now that you're here. So, are you going to tell us about who *you* fancy? If not Ash . . . then who?'

'OK, OK, I'll tell you . . .'

Tara turns the lights low and I plug my laptop into the speakers and set my music on to shuffle, and we snuggle down under duvets, eating TimTam biscuits and sipping home-made milkshakes. I feel about five years old, but it's a nice feeling, warm and safe and good.

I tell Tara and Bennie about Riley, about the day at the beach and how the air practically sizzled between us, there was so much chemistry, but that the minute he heard my age he lost interest. When I tell them about the SpiderWeb add and the pre-dawn flirting, their eyes widen.

'Like a fantasy romance,' Bennie says.

It has occurred to me already that an Internet romance could be a lot less trouble than a real-life one – when you're chatting online, things can't escalate the way they do in the real world. I don't want my friends to think that Riley is

✿✿✿✿✿✿✿✿✿✿✿✿✿✿✿✿✿✿✿✿✿

just some kind of fantasy, though . . . that makes me look kind of sad.

'He's not a fantasy, he's real,' I point out. 'I've met him, remember?'

'Right,' Bennie says. 'And he's a student – how old, exactly?'

I shrug. 'Eighteen or nineteen, maybe? And gorgeous!'

'What's he studying?' Tara chips in. 'Which uni is he at?'

'I don't know,' I say. 'We don't talk about stuff like that. Is there more than one uni?'

'There's a whole bunch of them,' Bennie says. 'You'd think he'd have mentioned which. I wonder why he changed his mind about the age gap, decided it didn't matter after all?'

'He just did,' I say, irritated. 'A few years shouldn't make any difference. It's not like he's ancient!'

'No, obviously,' Bennie persists. 'But . . . a student wouldn't normally bother with a schoolgirl. Or have the patience for an online relationship, when he lives close by and could just meet up with you in real life if he wanted. It's a bit weird. You don't think he's got something to hide?'

✿✿✿✿✿✿✿✿✿✿✿✿✿✿✿✿✿✿✿✿✿✿

My irritation gives way to unease. Is Bennie right? Could Riley be playing games with me? I may have a thing for bad boys, but I don't want to be messed around.

Tara nudges Bennie in the ribs sharply.

'It's not weird, it's lovely!' she exclaims, flicking her newly short hair so that it swings around her face. 'A hundred years ago he'd have been wooing you with poems and flowers, and now it's SpiderWeb messages – it's just a different way of being romantic. I bet he does ask you out!'

'If he doesn't, I'll ask *him*,' I decide. 'I'll soon find out if he's serious or not!'

'Look,' Bennie says. 'I didn't mean to be negative. It just seems odd, that's all. And I was pretty sure you had a thing for Ash at the cafe because he definitely likes you!'

'He's cool,' I say. 'But so is Riley, and he's more of a challenge!'

Bennie shakes her head. 'I think you're crazy,' she says. 'Ash is gorgeous . . . and available! Still, your choice, obviously!'

I laugh and roll my eyes. 'Who knows, you could be right,' I concede. 'My taste in boys hasn't always been good, but I've had a lot of fun learning from my mistakes!'

❁❁❁❁❁❁❁❁❁❁❁❁❁❁❁❁❁❁❁❁

'Have you been in love lots of times?' Tara asks. 'Did anyone ever break your heart?'

'It goes with the territory,' I admit. 'Shall I show you some of my exes?' I reach across to the laptop and open up a new window, clicking through the photos I've uploaded from my iPhone. Tara and Bennie see split-second images of JJ, Marty, Phil, Joey, pictures of me before I scrubbed up and turned good-girl.

'Whoa,' Tara gasps as a photo of Kes comes up. 'Who's that?'

'Just an ex,' I say, rolling my eyes. 'He was trouble . . .'

'And you like trouble,' Bennie says with a grin.

'I'm trying to change,' I declare.

'Stick with us,' Tara says. 'We can keep you on the straight and narrow!'

I laugh because I know that actually nobody can keep me on the straight and narrow. God knows, Mum tried hard enough.

'What about the boy, though?' Bennie wants to know. 'Did he cheat on you? Did he break your heart?'

'He didn't cheat,' I explain. 'He didn't break my heart either – it was pretty much broken to start with. Kes was

❀❀❀❀❀❀❀❀❀❀❀❀❀❀❀❀❀❀❀❀❀❀❀❀

just one of a whole bunch of no-goods. I had a serious boyfriend a couple of years back, though . . . his name was Shay.'

I find a picture, an old one where he's laughing into the camera, beanie hat askew, guitar in hand.

'Awww,' Tara whispers. 'He's lovely!'

'What happened?' Bennie prompts.

I shrug, looking into the distance for maximum dramatic effect. 'My new stepsister stole him from right under my nose,' I say. 'She's still dating him. Can you imagine? I guess I lost my way for a little while. I made some bad choices, went off the rails, messed up at school. I'm not proud of it.'

My new friends are open-mouthed, soaking up this information. It's all true – it's just not the whole truth. Looking back, I know I took Shay for granted, but still, I loved him. I just didn't show it. As for the rest, the full details of my fall from grace at Exmoor High School are dull and sad and sordid. Even I don't blame Cherry for that. I close down the photo album abruptly.

'Whoa!' Tara says. 'I can't believe it. Who would do a thing like that to their own stepsister?'

❀❀❀❀❀❀❀❀❀❀❀❀❀❀❀❀❀❀❀❀❀❀❀

'You had to live with this girl?' Bennie checks. 'Without actually strangling her? Nightmare! Is that why you've come to live with your dad?'

'I couldn't stand it any more,' I say. 'I couldn't stay there.'

'No wonder!'

'That's why I'm taking things slow with Riley,' I add. 'And so an online flirtation seems . . . well, better, for now. I'm through with heartbreak.' Plus, of course, Dad has made it very clear he doesn't want me seeing anyone. I don't mention that bit, though.

My new friends nod, a little awestruck, as if I am some exotic creature that escaped from a zoo, dangerous, fascinating, unpredictable.

The haircut verdict is almost unanimous. Tara's mum does not approve, but hey, it's only a haircut. She'd faint clean away if she knew just how much of a bad influence I could be if I *really* tried. Maybe she can sense it because she makes cinnamon toast for us the morning after the sleepover with her nostrils flared as if fire might blaze out of them at any moment. Truth is, though, Tara looks amazing; cute and quirky and mysterious, as if she has grown up overnight.

At school on Monday, the compliments come thick and fast. 'You look so different. Bet it cost a fortune! Where did you go? It totally suits you!'

Tara just smiles and flicks her hair and walks away, a new confidence wrapped round her like an invisible cloak. Best of all, Bennie reports that Joshua McGee walked up to Tara at the bus stop and said he liked her hair.

'It was the best moment of my entire life,' Tara breathes.

'She turned the colour of a beetroot,' Bennie adds. 'But she didn't run away. Progress, right?'

'Definite progress.'

What can I say? I am a genius.

 **Message:
Summerdaze**

Hi there, big sister.

It was so weird to see you on Skype the other week. It was like we could just reach out and touch you, only of course we couldn't. I miss you. December is not the easiest month for me; the kitchen smelt amazing tonight because Mum has been making Christmas pudding and Christmas cake and home-made mincemeat to give away as prezzies. I was helping and pretending to take it all in my stride but I don't like it – it's stressful, scary.

Why does Christmas have to be about selection boxes and chocolate yule logs and eating until you could burst? I am dreading it, Honey. I wish it could be how it was when we were little, when the only thing we worried about was whether it would snow or not, and whether we could stay awake until Father Christmas came. I really miss those days.

Summer xxx

11

I read Summer's message on my iPhone at lunchtime on Monday and my heart flips over. There are times when being in Australia feels like being on a whole different planet, and this is one of them. My sister needs me and I'm not there to help – that sucks. I tap out a quick reply.

> Summer, you are beautiful and clever and strong and you've come a long way since August. I don't think I've ever told you how proud I am of you, but I am . . . so proud.
> Christmas is going to be stressful. Food's everywhere, right? But food can't hurt you, little sister. It's not the enemy. This is just a wobble – everyone has them, even me. You think I've turned over a new leaf, ditched the drama queen strops? Think again. I mess up sometimes

– lots of times. But I am trying, and that's what counts.
I won't stop trying, and I know you won't either because
you are not a quitter, Summer Tanberry.
Love you lots,
xxx

After school, I stay back at study club with Tara and Bennie,
then waste a couple of hours window shopping and drinking smoothies in the local mall. It's a welcome distraction.
I need to speak to Mum alone, to tip her off that Summer
is struggling, but the time difference means I can't call
yet – everyone will be sleeping, and later my sisters will be
getting ready for school and it'll be chaos.

I miss that chaos sometimes. Back home I often had to
barricade myself into my bedroom to get a minute to
myself – you never knew what to expect from one minute
to the next. Skye might be making a dress out of the
bedroom curtains or playing crackly, ancient jazz records
on her gramophone; Summer could be practising *grand
jetés* in the hallway and Coco might be playing violin dirges
in the nearest treetop. Dad's house is quieter. He doesn't
get home till past seven o'clock and twice last week he
worked really late again. I felt a bit sorry for Emma, but

let's face it, I did not come to Sydney to hang out with my dad's girlfriend.

By the time I get home, Emma is setting the table and lighting candles in the dining room as Dad decants takeaway Indian food into fancy dishes and sets them in the oven to stay warm. Both of them are dressed up, Dad in a sharp suit and Emma in a blue satin slip-dress with a collar of pearls.

'Swit-swoo,' I say to Emma. 'What's going on?'

Dad glances up, frowning slightly, as if he's forgotten my existence. 'Client dinner,' he says. 'All very last minute. We need to just make one last push to clinch the deal, and I'm hoping that a friendly, family setting will help them see that we're the company to trust. I thought you were at a sleepover?'

'That was Saturday,' I tell him. 'Can I call home? I won't be long, promise. I need to talk to Mum. I'm a bit worried about Summer –'

Abruptly, Dad's fist slams down on to the kitchen table, making the empty takeaway cartons clatter and jump.

'Didn't you hear me?' he yells. 'I have important clients arriving any minute. Your sister is fine! All this fussing won't do her any good. You are in Sydney now, with me. You need to step away from Tanglewood, get on with your life!'

❀ ❀ ❀ ❀ ❀ ❀ ❀ ❀ ❀ ❀ ❀ ❀ ❀ ❀ ❀ ❀ ❀ ❀

The words feel like a slap, and my chin tilts up, defiant. 'You're saying I can't call home?' I challenge. 'Seriously?'

'I'm saying you can't use the landline,' Dad grates out. 'Seriously. Not now. It's not necessary and it's not convenient. You have a mobile, don't you? And a brand-new, top-of-the-range laptop, just a week or so old. Use them, if you really need to, but I won't have you disrupting this dinner party with some pointless telephone drama, all at my expense.'

I can't quite believe what I'm hearing. Pointless drama? Summer is falling to pieces back home and my dad doesn't even care.

Emma moves between us, trying to calm things down. 'Hey, hey, you two,' she says brightly, as if we are squabbling five-year-olds. 'No fighting! Honey doesn't mean it, do you, pet? Stop worrying and get your glad rags on and we'll have some fun –'

Dad turns on Emma. 'For goodness' sake, woman!' he growls. 'Can you take this seriously? It's bad enough that I've had to order food in because you're not able to cater for a straightforward dinner –'

'Greg!' she protests. 'This was a last-minute thing; there wasn't time to cook, you know that. I just thought –'

❀❀❀❀❀❀❀❀❀❀❀❀❀❀❀❀❀❀❀❀❀❀❀

'You didn't think at all,' Dad argues. 'Either of you. That's the whole trouble!'

I had forgotten Dad's temper, but suddenly the memories flood back – Dad storming out of the house and not returning for hours, or days; Mum crying; the rages that flared up out of nowhere and took the floor out from under our feet. I take two steps back, eyes wide, body tense. My hand closes on the bedroom door and I stumble backwards suddenly, away from the conflict. Dad glares at me.

'I'll stay in my room,' I whisper. 'OK? I wouldn't want to ruin your party.'

Emma's cheeks are pink with shame. She looks as if she might argue, but Dad doesn't give her a chance.

'Fine,' he snaps.

I close the door and throw myself down on the bed, shaking with shock and fury. How can Dad be so selfish, so unfair? Maybe I have seen his anger in the past but it has never been directed at me before. I never thought it could be. I was his golden girl, his princess . . . but he seems to have forgotten all that.

Someone switches on the CD player and I hear a car

draw up, then the sound of voices, laughter. It all sounds brittle, fake.

I take a deep breath and text Mum to check she's around and alone, then Skype her to explain about Summer's message, keeping my voice bright and steady. Mum says she will talk to the clinic right away, make sure Summer gets extra support.

'Try not to worry, Honey,' she says. 'They told us to expect the odd setback; it's part of the illness. Thanks for letting me know so quickly – and for being there for Summer when she needed to talk.'

I bite my lip. I wasn't there, was I? I was a million miles away.

I cut the call and at last the tears come. I am not sure they're for Dad and Emma; I think they are for Mum and me and my sisters, for long-ago rows I buried away so that I almost forgot they ever happened at all. But they did – I know they did.

I sit alone in the darkened room, listening to the music and chat drifting out from the dining room. You would never guess that half an hour ago, the air was crackling with anger and accusations. If you didn't know any better, you'd think this was the perfect dinner party, with bright, chatty, friendly people eating delicious food and listening to a Katie Melua CD.

If you didn't know any better, you'd think everything was just fine.

Charlotte Tanberry
<charlotte@chocolatebox.co.uk>
to me ✉

Honey, just to let you know I've spoken to the clinic;
they're confident they can help Summer. I could see
how upset you were when we spoke on Skype, but
try to stay strong, for Summer's sake. I'm glad she
could confide in you, and that you were smart
enough to let me know – you're growing up, sweetheart. I'm so proud you're making a go of your new
school, though right now I'd give anything to be
able to give you a hug, of course.
Love you lots,
Mum
xoxo

12

On Tuesday morning, Dad and Emma act like last night's blow-up never happened. If it wasn't for the lingering smell of vanilla candles, the empty wine bottles in the recycling bin and the dishwasher still steaming with sparkly clean plates and glasses, I'd think I dreamt the whole thing, but there is something too careful, too practised, about the way the two of them behave at breakfast. Dad is at his most helpful, squeezing fresh orange juice and making pancakes, but Emma's smile seems forced.

Dad's trying to make up for last night, I know, but although I smile and gulp down an orange juice I can't forget that shocking flash of anger and arrogance. I can be selfish and moody too, sometimes, but I'm not that bad, surely? Is this how scary it feels for my mum and sisters when I get mad? I can't even think about that.

School feels like a welcome retreat from the drama, and I lose myself in the dull routine of it. A surprise science test, a poem to analyse in English, a packed lunch eaten in the sunshine while talking about the rules of flirting with Tara and Bennie . . . these things seem valuable suddenly, small fragments of normality.

After school, I walk to the beach cafe to see Ash. He's busy serving drinks when I first arrive, so I pull up a bar stool and start on a two-page French essay about my life. Dutifully I look up a few useful phrases; my favourites are *demi-soeur de l'enfer* (stepsister from hell) and *délinquant juvénile* (you can guess that one, right?). Sadly, though, I am not sure Australia is ready for my life story; in the end I go for a slightly adapted version, where families are happy and not broken, and coming to Australia is a treat and not a punishment. It's not dishonest, exactly . . . it's just that it isn't the whole picture.

'Writing me a love letter?' Ash teases, and I laugh and tell him it's just French homework.

❀❀❀❀❀❀❀❀❀❀❀❀❀❀❀❀❀❀❀❀❀❀❀

'Speaking of love letters, though . . . my friend Tara has a little crush on you.'

'Not my type,' Ash says, serving iced coffees to a couple of elderly ladies before fixing a fruit smoothie for me.

'Bennie then?' I tease.

'She's great, but no,' he says. 'Spark's just not there.'

'No pleasing some people,' I say. 'What is your type, anyway?'

'I'll tell you some time. Maybe.' His eyes snag mine then slide away, and both of us are smiling. Ash likes me, I know he does, and even though his kind, hardworking boy-next-door style is a million miles from my own usual type, my heart still races a little bit whenever I'm with him.

'Is it weird to be so far away from your mum and sisters?' he asks, and the comment feels a little too close to home; my mind has been on Summer all day.

'It must be tough. How do you get your head around it?' Ash pushes, and like a fool I open my mouth and let the truth spill out.

'I don't. Sometimes – I guess since my parents split up – I feel as if I've been divided into pieces, like a jigsaw.

134

❀❀❀❀❀❀❀❀❀❀❀❀❀❀❀❀❀❀❀❀❀❀❀

I don't know if I can ever feel complete until all the pieces are joined up.'

'Think it'll ever happen?' he asks.

'No chance. Jigsaws are going out of fashion – nobody has the patience for them any more. I am destined to wander around for the rest of my days with bits missing everywhere . . .'

I hold a hand up, faking a horrified look, as if I can see right through it.

'Everything's where it ought to be from where I'm standing,' he says, raising an eyebrow. 'No jigsaw-shaped gaps.'

'I hide them well,' I quip. 'And it's ironic, but if I work hard, I kind of forget what a mess my life is! Blaming you for that, Ash. I've never had a work ethic before!'

Ash laughs. 'The hard work will be worth it,' he says. 'It's a way of opening up the future – you'll see!'

'I'm not thinking about the future so much as trying to keep my head above water,' I admit. 'What about you?'

Ash grins. 'I want to get good grades in my Higher School Cert, then travel . . . do a gap year before uni. Then I might study journalism and end up being a war correspondent or a teacher or a writer. I'm still deciding.'

135

❀❀❀❀❀❀❀❀❀❀❀❀❀❀❀❀❀❀❀❀❀❀

'I'd like to jump off the whole treadmill the moment I can,' I admit. 'I hate school. I think I'm allergic to rules and uniform and homework. And exams.'

Ash raises an eyebrow. 'You've always got your nose in a book; I don't see it bringing you out in a rash exactly.'

'I have a lot to catch up with,' I tell him. 'I wasn't an A-star student back home, and the syllabus is different here, so I'm way behind. I'd like to prove I can do it, but what can I say? I get bored easily, and my biggest talent is chaos. Some days I feel like a runaway train, no brakes, no nothing. It's just a matter of time until I plough right off the tracks . . .'

'Train crashes aside, what would you really like to do?' he asks. 'If there were no school, no exams?'

There are a million smart answers to that, answers involving all-night parties, unsuitable boys, London bedsits, rags-to-riches fantasy stories. Trouble is, I can't summon up much enthusiasm for any of it, and my smart answers evaporate, leaving me with nothing.

'I like to draw,' I say, surprising even myself. 'Apart from chaos, it's the only thing I'm any good at.'

'Art college then?'

136

'What are you, my personal tutor?' I tease. 'We'll see. How about you? Where will you go on your gap year?'

Ash laughs. 'There's so much of the world I want to see – Sri Lanka, where my family were from originally, and Britain because . . . well, it just seems so cool. I'd like to see for myself if it actually is!'

'Don't go to Somerset,' I warn him. 'I grew up there, and it's the land that time forgot.'

'You say that like it's a bad thing,' he says. 'It sounds kind of awesome.'

'Tanglewood *is* awesome,' I concede. 'In a quiet, sleepy kind of way. It's really cold there now, according to my sisters. Coco says there's frost on the grass most mornings . . .'

'I'd love to see it!'

'They shot a TV film right next to where we live, a few months back,' I say. 'If you want to see what the place looks like. Coco and I were extras – we had to dress as Edwardians and wander about in the background while the real actors did their stuff. The film's airing in the UK tomorrow night, so by Thursday I'll be able to see it on *Watch-Again* . . .'

137

'No kidding,' Ash says. 'I'm talking to a movie star?'

I shrug. 'You know me, full of surprises.' I feel a sudden impulse to get closer to Ash – he makes me want to confide in him, trust him. Could it be he understands me properly, that maybe, just maybe, boy-next-door *is* my type after all? 'You can watch it with me, if you want!' I add as casually as I can.

Just then, a group of teenage girls crowd the counter, bombarding Ash with a complicated list of requests for smoothies and ice cream. He heads for the fridge, raking a hand through his hair.

'Look, I can't do the film thing on Thursday,' he calls over to me. 'I'm busy.'

Ash has told me how uneventful his life is outside work, so how come he's suddenly tied up the minute I suggest something? I'm not used to boys saying no to me; it's not even as if I was asking him on a date or anything. Not exactly. What if he already has a girlfriend? My mates fancy him, and the teen girls flirting away as he lines up multiple smoothies and sundaes seem to feel the same way.

Hurt curdles inside me, but I fix a smile into place.

'No worries,' I call back, sweeping school books

awkwardly into my bag. 'I'd better go, tons to do, you know how it is.'

Ash calls after me as I push my way out of the cafe, but I don't look back; my eyes are stinging, as if I might cry, and I really, really don't want him to see that.

The next morning I wake at four, as if some internal alarm clock has started shrieking in my head. I pull the pillow over my head and grit my teeth, but images of yesterday fill my head, images of Ash looking awkward, his eyes sliding away from mine.

I feel so stupid for asking him to watch the TV film with me; I wanted him to see the place where I grew up, and yes, I wanted him to see me the way I looked that day, wearing a beautiful vintage dress, my hair and make-up carefully styled. The trouble with letting people get close to you is that they turn round and hurt you. My dad did it, Shay did it . . . you think I'd learn.

Even Riley has gone cold on me again. He hasn't messaged once since our conversation on Friday morning, and I haven't messaged him – I have some pride. It's pretty much all I do have, along with my best friend Jet Lag.

❀❀❀❀❀❀❀❀❀❀❀❀❀❀❀❀❀❀❀❀❀❀❀

I shove the pillow away, ignore the pile of school books and open up my laptop.

I type a message.

Riley? You around? How come you've gone all silent on me lately?
xxx

I press Send, then swear under my breath. It's too late to regret it now; the message has gone, lost in the nothingness of the Internet. My heart flips over as a message appears in my inbox.

Honey? What's up?

My cheeks colour. He's online, but he hasn't messaged me, even though he knows I'm always awake at this time. Shame seeps through me.

Nothing much . . . just wondered what you were up to.

I'm trying for a light, banter-ish tone, but I'm not sure it's working. An answer comes back almost at once.

❁❁❁❁❁❁❁❁❁❁❁❁❁❁❁❁❁❁❁❁❁

> Busy with uni work. Had a couple of deadlines, you know the kind of thing. What's going on with you?

The message is a world away from our flirty chats last week. I don't know what I've done wrong, but I can feel Riley's interest ebbing away like the ocean when the tide turns. Bennie's right – maybe you really can't have a relationship on social media. You need to hang out together, chat, laugh, hold hands. If I could see Riley, I could keep him interested, I know I could. With just words to work with, it's not so easy.

I think quickly before I reply.

> Things are cool. Waiting to see my small-screen debut this week. I was an extra in a TV film a while ago, back home. It's being screened in Britain tonight and it's on *Watch-Again* tomorrow . . . weird, huh?
> xxx

A minute later, an answer appears.

> You're a movie star? Serious? Wish I could see that!

I smile. Riley is way more enthusiastic than Ash was, and that's an ego boost if nothing else. Do I dare ask *him* over?

❀❀❀❀❀❀❀❀❀❀❀❀❀❀❀❀❀❀❀❀❀❀❀❀❀❀❀

How fine a line is there between brave and desperate? My new-leaf promises crumble to nothing as my fingers fly over the keyboard.

> You could come over and watch it with me, if you like . . .
> xxx

I hold my breath, and an answer appears.

> Sure! I don't have lectures tomorrow, so tell me your address and I'll come once you've finished school. Give me your mobile too, just in case.

I grin, typing out my address and mobile number. My inbox flashes up with a reply.

> Cool! See you soon, gorgeous!

I pick up my pillow from the floor and hug it tight, smiling in the half-light.

Coco Tanberry

<coolcoco@chocolatebox.co.uk>

to me ✉

We just watched *Scarlet Ribbons* and I really, honestly think we might be famous now! Me and Humbug were in a few scenes, in the background, but there were quite a few close-ups of you, Honey Tanberry. How cool?

Your Fellow Film Star,

Coco x

13

The next thirty-six hours stretch out to an eternity. I play it cool, but let's face it, I'm not the patient kind, and it's way too long since I've had a date with a cute boy.

Tara and Bennie are fizzing with excitement, like two boisterous puppy dogs.

'I think I got this whole Riley thing wrong,' Bennie says. 'He's obviously mad about you!'

'Chemistry,' Tara breathes.

'You'd know all about that,' Bennie cuts in. 'There was a whole lot of *that* going on this morning between you and Joshua McGee!'

'You'd have been proud,' Tara says. 'I didn't blush crimson this time. More of a deep cerise colour. Anyhow, Bennie, you're just jealous!'

'Possibly,' she agrees. 'Ask Riley if he's got a friend for me, OK?'

'I might just do that!'

'Did he message again this morning?'

'Yep . . . says he can't wait,' I report. 'Nor can I. He's so good-looking, honestly!'

'Bring him into town on Saturday,' Bennie suggests. 'You can take him to that cafe where we went the other week, and Tara and I will just happen to stroll in. If he's as hot as you say, it'd be rude to keep him all to yourself.'

'I wish we could watch that film with you,' Tara says. 'I'm going to watch it anyway, and see if I can spot your sister, and listen out for Shay's song in the soundtrack . . .'

'Text us the minute Riley's gone,' Bennie adds. 'We want to know *all* the details. Don't hold back!'

'I won't,' I promise, laughing.

I'm not laughing at four 'o clock, though. I'm back home, peeling off the tent dress, jumping into the shower, dressing quickly in a little print sundress and flip-flops. Emma lends me her hairdryer and I do my make-up, my hand shaking slightly as I apply eyeliner.

'You look fabulous,' Emma says. 'I've got you some pizza

and dips, and a bag of salted caramel popcorn. Boys like that sort of thing. When he comes, I'll say hello and then pop across the road for a coffee with Josie. If you need me you know where I am. Your dad's working late again tonight, so that won't be a problem.'

'Emma, thanks!' I say, and I mean it. Emma has been brilliant since I told her about Riley's proposed visit yesterday afternoon, genuinely pleased that I am settling in and making friends. Last night we dragged the Christmas tree down from the loft, wrapped it in sparkly pink lights and hung Emma's designer glass ornaments on it – it looks like something out of a style magazine, seriously. Back home we have a real tree, lopsided, shedding needles, decorated with a million mismatched decorations made and accumulated over the years; it would never win any prizes for style.

'Your dad won't be too keen if he thinks this is a date,' Emma reminds me. 'He really does expect you to swear off boys for the next ten years, but you and I both know that isn't very fair. You're only human! I remember being fifteen . . . I used to fall in love every other day!'

'It's nothing like that,' I tell her. 'We hardly know each

146

other. We're just . . . friends.' I cross my fingers behind my back and hope for the best.

'If you say so,' Emma says. 'Still, it's nice to see you having some fun. Greg has been a bit stressed lately, with lots of big contracts on the line at work, but I know he thinks the world of you. He's just not used to having a teenager around.'

I blink, speechless. I do not want apologies and excuses from Emma for my dad's angry outburst, no matter how well-meaning.

'When I told Greg you had a friend coming over, I think he assumed it would be a girl,' Emma goes on. 'We don't need to tell him any different! You can watch the film in the living room, so everything's out in the open and above board.'

'Oh . . . can't we just watch it in my room?'

Emma squeezes my arm. 'It's not that I don't trust you,' she says. 'I do, of course, but I think it's best to keep things light and friendly. As you said, you don't know each other well, and it might just give the wrong impression. Now, when did you say he was due?'

'He just said straight after school,' I say. 'He didn't give a specific time.'

❀❀❀❀❀❀❀❀❀❀❀❀❀❀❀❀❀❀❀❀❀❀❀

Emma smiles and I set my laptop up on the coffee table, checking the *Watch-Again* link. Once I'm happy it's all working properly, I plump up a few cushions on the cream leather sofa and open the popcorn and pour it into a bowl. Where is he?

I flick open a window on SpiderWeb in case Riley's sent a message, but there's nothing, so I flop down on to the sofa and pick up a handful of popcorn.

'He's travelling from the other side of the city,' I tell Emma. 'So, he could be a little bit late . . .'

'Where does he live exactly?' Emma asks.

'I'm not sure.'

'Is he coming by bus or by train? Or is he getting a lift?'

'I don't know. Look, Emma, why don't you just go over to Josie's? I'll send you a text when Riley gets here, if you like?'

'No, no, I don't mind waiting,' she insists. 'No trouble.'

When Riley hasn't shown up by half six, I'm struggling to keep my cool and Emma's expression has gone from excited to embarrassed, pitying. She says something kind about a mix-up with the times, and nips across the road to see her friend, leaving me alone with my shame. He hasn't

148

messaged or texted, and stupidly, although I gave him my mobile number, I didn't think of asking for his. Why would he say he was coming over and then not bother? Has he got the arrangements muddled? Or did something else come up, something more interesting than me?

Why did I even ask him? I've only met him once, for a couple of minutes; when I picture us together the images morph into memories of me and Shay from long ago. The early morning SpiderWeb chats have made me feel like I know him, but was any of that even real? Bennie was right – my relationship with Riley was all fantasy, just a SpiderWeb flirtation. I wish I'd left things that way; I wouldn't be feeling so let down now.

I'm still hurt that Ash turned me down too, although I'd never admit that to anyone.

I open my laptop and type.

Riley? What's up? Did I get the day wrong? Is everything OK?

I press Send, but there's no reply, no matter how many times I look.

❀❀❀❀❀❀❀❀❀❀❀❀❀❀❀❀❀❀❀❀❀❀

When Emma comes back at half eight, I pretend Riley messaged to cancel, and she puts an arm round my shoulders and tells me no boy is worth getting upset over. My mobile buzzes with the first of many messages from Tara and Bennie asking how things have gone; I switch it off and tell Emma I've got a headache, retreating to my bedroom. I curl up on the bed and stare blankly at the ceiling for hours, until I hear Dad's car pull up and the sound of the two of them talking.

He doesn't come in to see me, so I have no way of knowing what Emma has told him. My head is hurting and my heart aches with self-pity. I imagine Riley, drinking beer at some wild student party; and Ash, walking along a moonlit beach with some unknown girl.

What is it about me? What makes me so unlovable, so easy to walk away from? I wish I knew. Dad used to tell me I was his best girl, his princess, but that didn't matter one bit when he decided he'd stopped loving Mum. In the end, I wasn't wanted. I was left behind, thrown away like yesterday's rubbish, and the hurt inside me slowly turned to anger.

I've travelled halfway round the world to be with Dad.

I've worked my socks off at the dullest school in the known universe, stayed in almost every night, washed dishes, been nice to Emma and bitten my tongue every time I felt a snarky remark bubbling up to the surface. Well, almost every time. I've tried my hardest, but guess what? Dad still doesn't have time for me, even now we are living under the same roof.

I push the thought away; sometimes the truth hurts too much.

At midnight I eat cold pizza that tastes of cardboard and watch *Scarlet Ribbons* on *Watch-Again*, remembering the summer holidays at Tanglewood and the filming, when I still thought I could have it all, before I messed up one time too many. Watching myself in the movie is like watching a stranger – another version of me, brighter, braver, brimful of spiky, sassy backchat. I am wearing long petticoats and a cotton dress the colour of bluebells, my hair pinned up with fake plaits and a straw hat. It's like seeing some ghostly, past-life version of myself, someone long gone. When I look in the mirror now I can't see anything bright or brave or sassy. I just see a lost girl, someone who has run out of options. Can a person unravel so fast?

❁❁❁❁❁❁❁❁❁❁❁❁❁❁❁❁❁❁❁❁❁

I wish you could edit the past, delete the bits you don't want any more.

Kitnor looks beautiful in the movie, of course, with its lush, moss-green fields and little, twisty trees, its pebbled beaches stretching down to a silver sea. In the background, behind the real actors, I catch sight of people I know: Coco, dressed in a red pinafore, pulling Humbug the sheep on a lead; Finch, Skye's holiday romance; there's no Skye because she was working on the costumes behind the scenes, and no Summer because this was round about the time she started to get ill.

As the film ends, the credits go up and Shay's song 'Bitter-sweet', the song he wrote for Cherry, begins to play. It fits the mood of the film perfectly, and my mood too, with its talk of lost love and regrets.

Shay . . . he left me too, of course. I thought he'd always be there for me, but my new stepsister came along and stole him. 'I tried to make you happy,' Shay said when we broke up. 'I tried my hardest, but I can't, Honey – only you can do that. You're beautiful on the outside, but inside you're all eaten up with hurt. It's like some kind of poison. You have to stop being so angry, so destructive, so . . . lost. I can't cope with it any more.'

❀❀❀❀❀❀❀❀❀❀❀❀❀❀❀❀❀❀❀❀❀❀❀❀

He walked away, and what was left of my heart just crumbled.

Maybe Shay was right. Maybe inside I am all eaten up with poison, and nobody will ever love me. I lie awake most of the night, tossing and turning in the humid heat.

BennieJ

Hope it all went well and you're just not answering my texts because you're all loved up and happy. Can't wait to see you at school to get all the juicy details!
B xx

14

My messed-up, jet-lagged head decides to fall asleep just when everyone else is getting up, and I sleep through the alarm.

Emma shakes me awake at eight, and Dad calls out that he'll give me a lift to school if I can be ready in ten minutes flat. I dive into the shower, drag on my uniform, grab my bag and sprint out on to the driveway just as Dad is backing the car out. I realize I've forgotten my mobile and my pencil case, but too bad. I fall into the passenger seat and hook the seat belt across just as the door slams shut.

Any hopes of a nice father–daughter bonding moment after Dad's angry outburst the other night are quickly squashed.

'Planning, Honey,' Dad says, without a trace of irony.

'If you want your life to run smoothly, plan in advance and always allow enough time to get to where you want to be. These things make a difference.'

I try to smile, but it's not easy while applying lipgloss in a moving car and listening to Dad's life lessons at the same time.

Does he know how hard it is to listen to this kind of thing when your life is a train crash? *If you want your life to run smoothly, choose parents who stick together through thick and thin and boys who turn up when they say they will*, I think.

'Just a blip,' I say out loud. 'My sleep patterns are still out of sync – I had about an hour's sleep.'

'You look awful,' he says, and I sigh and pull out the concealer to wipe away the dark shadows under my eyes.

Dad brakes suddenly to let a van out from one of the side roads, and I drop the concealer and have to scrabble on the floor for it. As my fingers fumble around, they close on something small and cold and metallic, and I open my hand to reveal an earring, silver and expensive-looking with a red stone. Emma usually wears simple gold hoops, but she must have gone flash for a special night out.

❀❀❀❀❀❀❀❀❀❀❀❀❀❀❀❀❀❀❀❀❀❀

'Emma's lost an earring,' I say, holding it up.

Dad swerves the car in towards the kerb, a hundred metres away from the school gates.

'It's not Emma's,' he says, holding out his hand. 'I think it might belong to that Malaysian client Emma and I took out to dinner the other week. I'll see it's returned.'

A memory stirs, something niggling and just out of reach from long ago. The lost earring reminds me of something, but I can't figure out what.

'Honey? The earring?'

'Oh . . . right,' I say, handing it over. 'No worries. Thanks for the lift. See you later, Dad!'

School is agony. Tara and Bennie are lying in wait, demanding all the gossip on my date with Riley. I tell them that he didn't turn up, trying to turn it into a joke, but my eyes mist over as I speak and after that they treat me like some sort of injured kitten, to be stroked and protected and spoken to in hushed whispers. It makes me want to scream.

I stumble through the day as though I'm wading through porridge. My head is fuzzy from lack of sleep and wisps of memory tease me, hinting of something forgotten and

❀❀❀❀❀❀❀❀❀❀❀❀❀❀❀❀❀❀❀❀❀❀

significant. I just can't hang on to the thoughts for long enough to make sense of them.

Worse, something weird is going on with my classmates. It's not everyone, but a few of the girls are looking at me strangely, disapprovingly. It's like there's some kind of joke at my expense, only nobody is actually laughing.

'Did you blab about Riley?' I ask my friends. 'Because people are giving me some really odd looks.'

'Of course not,' Bennie frowns.

'We wouldn't,' Tara chimes in. 'Promise. There's always some silly rumour going around in this place, but it won't be anything to do with you.'

I can't help worrying, though. After study group, a couple of maths quiz girls, who have been quite friendly to me up till now, hang around on the school porch and tell Tara and Bennie there's a team meeting down at the beach cafe.

'OK,' Tara says. 'You coming, Honey?'

I'd rather go home and sleep for a week, but I don't get a chance to reply.

A girl called Liane, who sits next to me in art class, steps forward. 'Sorry,' she says, giving me the same slightly sneery look I've been getting all day. 'Quiz team people only. We're

discussing tactics for the Christmas quiz against the boys'
school. I know you have your own tactics for dealing with
boys, Honey, but in the maths quiz it's all about brains,
not sleaze.'

'Sorry?' I echo, slightly stunned. 'What did you just say?'

Liane raises an eyebrow, then turns to link arms with her
friends; they are already walking away.

'What just happened?' I ask Tara and Bennie. 'Do those
girls have a problem with me?'

'Ignore them,' Bennie says. 'They have a problem with
everyone!'

'I don't think she meant to be so rude,' Tara adds, looking baffled. 'She's just . . . tactless. We should go, if it's
about the maths quiz, but you should come too, Honey, no
matter what Liane says.'

I think there is more to this than a tactless comment. A
feeling of unease unfurls in my stomach, a feeling that's
been building all day. Something's wrong, but Liane's words
have stirred up the rebel in me. I'm not going to let some
crazy maths geek tell me what I can and can't do.

'I'll come,' I say. 'Who does she think she is? The cafe's
a public place!'

159

❀❀❀❀❀❀❀❀❀❀❀❀❀❀❀❀❀❀❀❀❀

We walk along to the beach together, and I try to shake off the foggy, muddled feeling that has plagued me all day. I'm listening to Tara and Bennie talk about how Liane is totally out of order when I zone out again, and the long-ago memories begin to link up. *We were driving home through the lanes near Tanglewood, after a picnic on the moors, everyone laughing and talking at once; getting out of the car, Coco held up an earring she'd found trapped in the corner of the back seat, a small gold hoop. The atmosphere turned frosty then, and later on, once we were safely in bed, an epic row blew up between Mum and Dad . . .*

'Honey?' Tara is saying, waving a hand in front of my face. 'Hello? You were miles away!'

We're at Sunset Beach, crossing the boardwalk that leads to the cafe.

'I was remembering something,' I tell her. 'From years ago. Nothing important really; something that happened this morning must have triggered it . . .'

'OK,' Tara says. 'Look, we'd better sit with Liane and the team. Are you coming over?'

'I don't think I'm very welcome somehow,' I reply. 'I'll see you after your meeting, OK?'

160

❀❀❀❀❀❀❀❀❀❀❀❀❀❀❀❀❀❀❀❀❀❀❀

'OK,' Bennie says with a grin. 'No flirting with Ash, mind!'

'As if!'

The chances of my flirting with Ash are actually zero after his brush-off the other day. Compared to Riley's rejection, it's fairly minor, but I seem to be missing a few layers of skin these days because it really hurt. I'd planned to ignore Ash and ditch my after-school trips to the cafe, but here I am again, just asking for trouble.

I dump my schoolbag on the counter. Ash is out on the veranda, delivering a tray of Cokes to Liane's gang amid lots of laughter and banter. I see Liane glance my way and I give her the fingers because it seems a little bit less childish than sticking my tongue out. She pretends not to see, which is even more childish in my opinion.

Ash comes back through, and when he sees me his face lights up. It's hard to stay frosty with him, but I do my best, and when he gets to the counter I tell him not to mess with my head because I am having a bad day and the last thing I need is more hassle.

'You're mad at me,' he says. 'Is it because I couldn't come over to see your film? Because I'd have loved to, only it just wasn't possible. Family stuff, y'know.'

'Tell me about it,' I reply. 'Or, actually, don't because I've had as much of it as I can take for one lifetime. OK?'

Ash holds his hands up. 'OK, OK . . . but I'm sorry, anyway. I would have explained, but I was serving about a million people at the time and you kind of stormed off. And then you vanished from the face of the earth. Thought I'd scared you away.'

'Trust me, you're the least of my troubles,' I say. 'So what if you don't want to hang out with me? Nobody else does either, not even my own family. At least you were upfront about it.'

'I do want to hang out with you,' Ash argues. 'I can't do evenings, that's all. I live with my sister and her husband, and they work regular night shifts at the hospital. I have to look after my nieces and nephew most nights. My life is pretty much school, then job, then babysitting, with occasional library visits shoehorned in. I have no social life at all, except for this place.'

I bite my lip. 'You were . . . babysitting?' I say. 'Honestly? It wasn't personal?'

'Why would it be personal?' he asks.

'Because my life is a disaster,' I tell him. 'And trust me,

it's always personal. I am just the kind of girl who attracts trouble. Everything I touch turns to dust.'

Ash laughs. 'That's rubbish,' he says, holding out his hand. 'Go on, try me . . . guaranteed not to turn to dust.'

'You don't understand!'

'I do,' he says. 'Go on, touch and see. I'm not trouble, and I'm not made out of dust. See?'

He presses his hand flat against my palm, warm and strong, and his fingers twine round mine, brown and white together. Nothing turns to dust except for the anger inside me. My heart beats hard. I look at Ash and his eyes hold mine for a long moment, and then I untangle my hand, untangle my eyes.

'I'll have a bit more time in the holidays,' he says carefully, 'if you still want to hang out. And I don't think you're trouble. Not at all.'

'You're wrong about that,' I say.

'I'm never wrong.'

I smile, and wonder why a boy like Ash who is serious and kind and hardworking would choose to believe in a girl like me, when hardly anybody else in the world does. It's a mystery.

'OK. If you're never wrong, explain this to me. If you find an earring in your dad's car and he says it doesn't belong to his girlfriend but to a client . . . would you believe him?'

Ash shrugs. 'Maybe. I guess it depends on your dad.'

'I guess so,' I tell him. 'Something about it's been bugging me all day. It reminded me of when Mum and Dad were still together, and my sister found an earring on the back seat of the car, and there was one almighty row. And a little while later, they split up.'

'Because of the earring?' Ash wants to know.

'No . . . well, possibly. I don't know. Perhaps Dad was having an affair. I was only eleven or twelve, I didn't really ask questions.'

An ancient surfer dude comes in to order a complicated baguette involving layers of ham, cheese, lettuce, tomatoes and pickle, and Ash takes a while to concentrate on the construction of it.

'Are you thinking that your dad could be seeing someone else now?' he asks carefully, once the surfer guy has gone. 'Like history is repeating itself? That's got to be tough.'

'He has been working late,' I consider. 'And there's a bit

of tension between him and Emma. Maybe that's what's bothering me. But I just keep thinking I've missed something . . . something obvious.'

Like history repeating itself, I think, and suddenly I understand. Dad really was having an affair back then, and that was why he and Mum divorced. I've spent a long time telling myself it was Mum's fault, but the facts were there all along; I just didn't want to see them.

A gold-hoop earring found in the car. A gold-hoop earring, the kind Emma likes to wear.

I grab my bag and head for the door.

'I have to go,' I call back to Ash. 'Tell Tara and Bennie something came up.'

I head out across the boardwalk and on to the sand, and then I break into a run.

Notifications

There are eleven new text messages,
six missed calls and two voicemail
messages for honeyb@chocolatebox.co.uk

15

I feel like I've stepped into a parallel universe. There's a huge bouquet of cellophane-wrapped red roses in the kitchen and Emma is dressed up in a pretty dress and silver spike-heel shoes.

Emma, kind, friendly Emma, who put an arm round my shoulder last night and told me no boy was worth getting upset over. Emma, who had an affair with my dad and broke up his marriage.

'Aren't they gorgeous?' she smiles, oblivious. 'Greg loves to surprise me with flowers, and he's booked a table at this new super-posh restaurant in town to make up for working late so much recently! We're doing an early dinner and then a show . . . isn't that cute?'

'Cute,' I echo coldly.

'Will you be OK?' Emma asks. 'On your own? I've left

❀❀❀❀❀❀❀❀❀❀❀❀❀❀❀❀❀❀❀❀❀❀❀❀

some cash in case you fancy takeaway pizza. Greg's swinging by in ten minutes to pick me up.'

'I'll be fine,' I say. 'How long have you and Dad been seeing each other, Emma?'

Her smile falters. 'A good while now . . . not too long after he split up with your mum, I think. Why do you ask?'

'Just wondered,' I say with a shrug. 'How did you meet?'

'Oh . . . well . . . I was your dad's Personal Assistant back at the London office, for years, really. So we were already good friends, and after they separated things just sort of took off . . .'

I bet they did.

'After the split?' I challenge. 'Definitely?'

Emma's cheeks darken, and she can't meet my eye. 'Look, Honey – this is ancient history. Why rake up the past?'

I am certain it wasn't after they broke up. I look at Emma, her glossy hair pinned up prettily to show off the signature gold-hoop earrings, and I wonder if she knows that a lost earring found in a car can change people's lives. I wonder if she knows that it happened back then, and that maybe it's happening again right now. I wonder if she cares.

❀❀❀❀❀❀❀❀❀❀❀❀❀❀❀❀❀❀❀❀❀❀❀

They say that what goes around comes around, but in spite of everything, I can't find it in me to hate Emma. There's the sound of tyres crunching on gravel. Dad toots the car horn and Emma hugs me and runs out of the house, and I'm left alone.

I fetch my mobile and laptop from the bedroom and stretch out on the sofa; there's an avalanche of notifications. Before I can click on to SpiderWeb, my iPhone buzzes with a new message.

Coco Tanberry
<coolcoco@chocolatebox.co.uk>
to me ✉

What are you PLAYING at, Honey? You are SO embarrassing! Get rid of the pic – it's tacky, even for you.

My heart starts to race. I type back, asking Coco what she's talking about. Seconds later, a one-word answer appears on the screen.

SpiderWeb.

✿✿✿✿✿✿✿✿✿✿✿✿✿✿✿✿✿✿✿✿✿✿✿

I click on to my home page and suddenly the whole day of funny, sideways looks begins to make sense. There on my home page is a photo of me, taken back in the spring at someone's party. It's a jokey, flirty picture of me leaning in to the camera, blowing a kiss and showing a little too much cleavage; but that's not the worst of it. The status printed above it makes me feel sick.

Feeling lonely . . . going to an all-girls' school sucks. Any cute boys out there want to help cheer me up?

I scan down. There are dozens of replies, some from girls at school telling me I should be ashamed, calling me disgusting names. It's the comments from boys – and men – that get me, though. Comment after comment, sleazy, saddo remarks from blokes offering to help cure my loneliness. And they leave me in no doubt about how they are planning to do that.

Amongst the sleaze, one comment stands out, from Surfie16.

Wish I'd made the effort to come along to see you last night now. Looks like there was a lot more on offer than the movie!

❀❀❀❀❀❀❀❀❀❀❀❀❀❀❀❀❀❀❀❀❀❀

Tears sting my eyes. How can you be so wrong about someone?

I don't even know half of these people . . . most of the names aren't on my friends list. As for the picture, it's an old one from my iPhone; when I got the laptop, I uploaded all of my mobile pictures and stored them in my Spider-Web photo albums, but I locked the privacy settings so that only I could access them. And I *know* I didn't post that picture on to my home page . . . so how did it get there?

I click Delete, and the post disappears.

No wonder the girls at school were acting strangely. No wonder Liane made her 'sleaze' comment. Even my little sister has seen the post, and the thought of that makes me sick with shame. I close my eyes, trying to make sense of it all and failing miserably. When I open my eyes again, a new private message from Surfie16 blinks at me from my inbox.

Hey . . . why'd you take the photo down? I liked it! You still lonely? Bet I can put a smile on your face!

I wipe away furious tears as I type.

✿✿✿✿✿✿✿✿✿✿✿✿✿✿✿✿✿✿✿✿✿✿

For God's sake – I didn't post that photo. I've no idea how it got there!

A reply appears a few moments later.

Well, it didn't get there all by itself, did it? Were you drunk last night or something? Missing me? ;o)

I grit my teeth.

No, I wasn't drunk and I didn't post it! Don't be such a slimeball, Riley!

Another message appears.

Don't be mad at me. OK, I stood you up – my bad. But why get so upset about a photo?

I literally growl at this. Is Riley stupid? I try to explain.

That picture was in a private folder. I don't see how anyone could have even known it was there, let alone post it online. All those awful comments . . . the girls at school think I'm sleazy and attention-seeking, and I seriously don't know who the guys who commented even are. I think I've been hacked!

A minute later, Riley's reply appears.

Check your security settings. If you haven't set them properly, everyone on your friends' SpiderWeb pages can see what you've posted and comment.

I am certain I put tight security settings in place when I created the page, but when I go to check the security is set so that 'everyone' can see what I post. I change it back to 'friends only' and check the settings on my photo albums – they too are set so that 'everyone' can see. Horrified, I ramp up the security again and click Save.

I type another message.

My security settings have changed. How can that happen?

A reply appears a few minutes later.

Guess you didn't set them right to start with. This was the kind of picture that attracts a lot of attention, but

✿✿✿✿✿✿✿✿✿✿✿✿✿✿✿✿✿✿✿✿✿✿✿

you should have thought about that before you put it
online.

Exasperated, I send off my response.

I didn't put the picture online! Why won't you believe
me?

There's no reply.

Message:
BennieJ

Thought I should let you know that Liane was saying some pretty nasty stuff about you after the meeting. Something about a picture on your SpiderWeb page, although when she tried to show us there was nothing there, so maybe she made it all up? Ash said you had to head off – hope everything's OK.

Bennie xxx

16

It takes forever to explain it all to Tara and Bennie. Luckily neither of them actually saw the photograph – I must have deleted it just in time – but Liane told them in great detail just how cringey it was. Great.

'Be careful next time,' Bennie says when we meet in town. 'I know you didn't mean anything bad, but some things are better kept private.'

'I didn't post it,' I say for what feels like the millionth time. 'I don't know how it got there, but it had nothing to do with me!'

Tara frowns. 'Are you saying it wasn't your picture?'

'It was an old one,' I explain. 'Taken at a party in April or May. I was messing around, having fun, and someone picked up my iPhone and took the picture. It was in a

❀❀❀❀❀❀❀❀❀❀❀❀❀❀❀❀❀❀❀❀❀❀❀

private SpiderWeb album – I'd never have posted it so people could see. Especially not with a comment like that.'

'Sounds like every lowlife on the Internet chipped in with something to say,' Bennie adds. 'Yuk.'

'Liane and some girls from school commented too,' I say. 'Think I've lost a few friends over this.'

'If they judge you over a stupid mistake –'

'Not a mistake,' I argue. 'I was hacked!'

'Well, whatever,' Tara says. 'If they were really your friends, they'd understand, that's all. Hold your head up, pretend nothing happened – scandals come and go at Willowbank. By next term, nobody will even remember.'

I'm not sure that's true; overnight five or six girls from school have vanished from my SpiderWeb. I don't think they see me as cool and exotic any more – more cheap and sleazy.

'We're on your side,' Tara says. 'Bennie stuck up for you when Liane was being spiteful. We've decided to drop out of the quiz team, for now at least. Friends are more important.'

I smile, touched at their loyalty.

'Do you really think you were hacked?' Bennie asks. 'Because if you did post the picture, because you were feeling

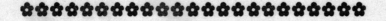

down about Riley not turning up or something . . . well, we'd understand. Everyone gets stuff wrong sometimes.'

'Me more than most,' I admit. 'But I didn't do this, Bennie. And I can't figure out who would.'

She considers. 'Who else has had access to your laptop? Or your iPhone even?'

I bite my lip. 'Just you two, really,' I say. 'At the sleepover. And I know you didn't even go near it, except when I was showing you those photos of Kes and Shay. Dad and Emma, of course . . . but they'd never do something like this. I've had my iPhone at school, though, and at the beach cafe.'

'Ash wouldn't,' Tara says firmly. 'He's OK.'

'And we wouldn't,' Bennie adds. 'You know that, obviously.'

'Obviously,' I agree. 'Maybe someone at school, but I know I haven't left my mobile out of sight, so I've no idea how!'

The more I think about it, the clearer it seems that some-one close to me is the culprit. And that really is scary.

I am literally counting down the days until school closes for the Christmas break, but despite the sweltering Aussie heat, the atmosphere in class is frosty. Not too many people actually saw the photo; we're not supposed to use mobiles

178

during the school day, but Liane has made sure everyone knows about it, and they all have an opinion.

I do a pretty good job of ignoring the nasty looks, but on Tuesday I end up stuck next to Liane in art. The mirrors we're using for our self-portrait paintings have been individually set up with leafy plants and still-life objects and draped fabric; they sit on the side benches from week to week, so we can go on with our paintings without delay or interruption. Moving is not an option, so I look straight through Liane as if she's not there at all. It takes some willpower, trust me.

Halfway through class Miss Kelly stops beside me, study-ing my picture. My brush freezes in mid-air, partway through painting the highlights on a piece of velvet draped from the top of the mirror.

'Have you used acrylic paint before, Honey?' she asks.

'No,' I admit. 'Why? Am I doing it wrong?'

Miss Kelly laughs. 'No, far from it! This self-portrait is expressive, powerful – quite extraordinary. The eyes . . . so sad and vulnerable and lost!'

I flinch at her words. Is that what people see when they look at this picture? At me? Shame floods my body like acid, eating away at me from inside.

❀❀❀❀❀❀❀❀❀❀❀❀❀❀❀❀❀❀❀❀❀❀❀

'So you don't have acrylic paints at home?' Miss Kelly is asking.

'No, Miss.'

'I'll find you a set of them to borrow over the holidays. I'd love to see more work like this, Honey. Perhaps some portraits of your family? You could make it a holiday project, build up your coursework folder.'

My family? I don't think so.

'Can I do something else, Miss?' I ask. 'Something less . . . personal?'

Miss Kelly laughs. 'Personal is what I want from you,' she says. 'Sometimes the most challenging tasks are the ones we learn most from!'

I try to argue, but when I open my mouth, nothing comes out. Miss Kelly moves on to help someone else.

She is my favourite teacher at Willowbank, gentle, kind, encouraging. Doesn't she know about my past? Does she want me to dig into all that, stir it up and turn it into art? My parents' marriage, smashed carelessly to bits by the woman who has made me feel welcome in Sydney; my boyfriend-stealing stepsister, Cherry; Paddy with his smug, sickly sweet dreams of happy-ever-after; even Dad, with his late nights and date nights and secrets. All of that would make great material for an art project. Not.

Miss Kelly hasn't a clue about any of this, though, because Dad has smoothed out the past, papered over the cracks, supplied a new story to explain my sudden appearance in Australia. I have even helped him do it.

Miss Kelly wants a project on family? I'll give her one, but it won't be the neat series of portraits she's expecting. I look into the mirror, and the eyes that meet mine aren't sad; they flash with fury.

Good. I like them that way.

Then I look at the painting, and there is the sadness Miss Kelly was talking about; wide blue eyes holding all the pain in the world. I don't want to see that, and I really, really don't want anyone else to. It feels like being stripped bare in the middle of the street.

'What's the matter, Honey?' Liane sneers, her face spiteful and sour. 'Not keen on the idea of family portraits? Guess the only person you like looking at is *you*, right? Only usually with much sluttier clothes on –'

A wave of anger threatens to engulf me. In one quick movement, I reach out and tip over the water jar, spilling

❀❀❀❀❀❀❀❀❀❀❀❀❀❀❀❀❀❀❀❀❀❀

muddy liquid all over the picture and all over Liane, who jumps up screaming. I grab the drawing board, dragging the waterlogged painting off it as if to rescue it; I'm not rescuing it, though – just the opposite. Miss Kelly turns to see Liane howling and yelling at me as the whole picture tears in half.

'Liane!' Miss Kelly cries. 'What have you done?'

'Me?' she screeches, outraged. 'It was Honey! She tipped water all over me and then ripped the picture in two! She's crazy!'

'I find it hard to believe she'd destroy her own painting,' the teacher says. She rushes to help, promising repairs and rescue. It's too late by then, though; I have dragged the damaged picture from the board, scrunched it up and thrown it into the bin.

'Honey!' she says. 'Your beautiful painting!'

'It was an accident!' I wail, wiping away an imaginary tear. 'I spilt the water. Liane was furious, but I don't blame her and I'm sure she didn't *mean* to do it –'

'I didn't do it at all!' Liane protests, but even her friends look doubtful. She doesn't like me; she's made that very clear. And now she looks like a jealous, vindictive bully, while

I seem more of a hapless victim with a very forgiving nature.

Liane glances at me, simmering with fury, but I just smile and say sweetly that I'm really, really sorry about her dress.

It's a pity they don't do drama lessons at Willowbank. I'd get top marks.

After school, I sit on a tall stool at the beach-cafe counter and confess all to Ash. 'She'd have been sent to Birdie if I hadn't pleaded for mercy on her behalf,' I recount with relish. 'I thought she was going to explode with fury. I guess that'll teach her to mess with me. See, Ash? I told you I wasn't very nice.'

He raises an eyebrow. 'Sounds like she kind of asked for it,' he says. 'Spreading rumours and bitching behind your back. But you're the loser, Honey. You destroyed your own painting. Why would you do that?'

I bite my lip. The truth is I ruined my picture because Miss Kelly said it made me look sad and vulnerable and lost. It gave too much away.

'I didn't like it,' I say carelessly.

Ash shakes his head. He is putting together a complicated ice-cream sundae involving layers of strawberries, peach slices and lots of ice cream – he thinks I need cheering up. He

183

finishes it off with a handful of chopped nuts, sugar sprinkles and a drizzle of strawberry sauce, a paper parasol perched on top.

'This should make you smile,' he says. 'On the house, of course.'

'You can't keep giving me free ice creams,' I tell him. 'You'll get into trouble.'

'I'm paying for them with my own money,' he says with a shrug. 'You're worth it.'

'You don't know anything about me,' I say darkly. 'Most people think I'm not worth it at all.'

'I'm not most people,' he replies. 'Besides, I've seen what can happen when someone gets on the wrong side of you!'

I sigh. Ash is definitely not like most people, but is that good or bad? I've only known him for a little while, yet I feel closer to him than anyone else in Sydney, even my elusive dad. But do I really know him? Can I trust him? Is he the kind of person who could hack into a phone and post flirty pictures and stupid comments? I don't think so, but it's hard to be sure.

He pushes the sundae dish over to me. 'What's up?' he asks. 'Is it just this Liane girl, or is something else going on?'

❀❀❀❀❀❀❀❀❀❀❀❀❀❀❀❀❀❀❀❀❀❀❀

'It's everything,' I say. 'Home, school, you name it. It's not just Liane who's being a pain – half the girls in my year are blanking me because of some stupid SpiderWeb post that appeared on my page. I know I don't have you on SpiderWeb, but . . .'

'I don't have it,' Ash says.

'No? I thought everybody did these days!'

'Not me,' Ash says. 'No laptop, no smartphone, just an ancient computer I share with everyone else in the house. Even getting to use it for school stuff takes planning, so . . . no SpiderWeb.'

'You could get a smartphone, surely?' I say. 'You work loads of shifts. You must have money saved.'

'I'm saving for a plane ticket around the world,' he reminds me. 'Gap year, yeah? I'd rather have a real life than an Internet one.'

I remember that not so long ago I was too busy breaking rules and staying out all night to bother much with Spider-Web myself. It seems like a lifetime ago.

'It's just a way of staying in touch with my sisters,' I explain. 'And with friends . . . old ones and new ones.' Not that I have many of either variety, sadly.

'Cool,' Ash says. 'Do you take friend applications from people not on SpiderWeb? If they have good ice-cream sundae skills?'

I grin, scooping up a spoonful of cream and strawberries. 'Might do,' I say.

'Will I see you over the holidays?' he asks, a little too casually. 'I'll be working different shifts, but I'll be here most days . . .'

I have a feeling I will too.

Summer Tanberry
<summerdaze@chocolatebox.co.uk>
to me ✉

Just to let you know your Christmas parcel arrived
yesterday . . . whoop! We have put the presents
under the tree and Coco has already poked and
prodded hers so much I've had to repair the holes
with Sellotape. Doing a little bit better with the food
stuff.
Love you, big sister.
xxx

To Honey!
Don't open these until
our Skype call, please!
Love from
xxx EVERYONE xxx

17

I have sung carols in the snow a few times, risking frostbite in fingerless mittens as I clutched the songbook, but I have never before dodged heatstroke while singing 'Little Donkey'. I guess there is a first time for everything.

We break up from school, and I try to get into the Aussie Christmas spirit. I drape fairy lights along the patio and hang up cards with surfing Santas, cards with sleighs drawn by kangaroos, cards with koalas wearing reindeer antlers. It's kind of surreal. I surprise Emma by teaching her how to bake mince pies and Christmas cake; we have a laugh, but the rich fruit-and-brandy aroma as the cake cooks makes me suddenly, painfully, homesick.

An airmail package addressed to me arrives from home, tied up with string and covered in Christmas stickers; I slice open the box and take out the presents inside, carefully wrapped in white tissue paper with red ric-rac bows. I read the gift-tag messages from my sisters, telling me not to open anything until my Skype call home on Christmas Day, and my throat aches suddenly, as if I've swallowed a shard of glass.

The day before Christmas Eve Bennie has a sleepover and we watch cheesy festive DVDs and exchange presents, promising not to open them until Christmas Day; we talk about our plans to hang out at the beach and meet cool boys.

'We have the whole of January to have fun,' I tell them. 'I can't wait!'

'About that,' Tara says. 'I didn't know how to tell you before, but Dad says he's taking us down to the Gold Coast right after New Year for a fortnight's holiday, then on to Brisbane for my Aunt Lisa's wedding. I'm looking forward to it, but I'll miss hanging out with you guys. And the cool boys bit, naturally . . .'

'All the more for us,' Bennie teases.

I'm sorry Tara will be away, but still, I can't help looking forward to the holidays. Forget the promises I made to Dad – a little bit of romance is exactly what I need right now. As I drift off to sleep I'm not thinking of Riley, with his surf-boy good looks and his hot/cold messages that have fizzled away to nothing. I'm thinking of Ash, with his books and his grin and the way his eyes hold on to mine whenever we're together. I've hardly managed to see him since school broke up – I can't seem to work out his new shift schedule, but I realize I miss him.

Last year I woke on Christmas morning with Coco jumping up and down on my bed like a maniac, trying to wake me. This year is different. There is no annoying stepdad playing cheesy carols on his fiddle; no bleary-eyed sisters eating chocolate coins and tangerines at six in the morning in front of a log fire; no ancient handknitted stockings hanging from the mantlepiece, bulging with tiny presents. There is just the stillness of the pre-dawn house, the sound of my own breathing.

Christmas morning is not meant for lie-ins, it's meant for barking dogs and footprints in the soot around the fireplace and wrapping paper torn carelessly to reveal those silly, lovely stocking presents you didn't even know you wanted. What will my sisters be doing now? Mum said they weren't having the usual Christmas Eve party . . . too much bother, she said, after all the hard work at the chocolate workshop these last few months. Too stressful for Summer too.

Will they be down in the village at a carol concert? Watching *It's A Wonderful Life*, that mad old black-and-white DVD about an angel earning his wings that Mum loves so much? Setting out a mince pie, a glass of whisky and a carrot for Rudolf, hanging up the stockings? It is 5.05 a.m. in Sydney, and Christmas has begun, but back home at Tanglewood it's still Christmas Eve. I am a time traveller, lost and far from home, drifting in the nowhere-land of darkness.

I open up my laptop, click on to SpiderWeb. There's a whole bunch of notifications; the first, surprisingly, is from Surfie16.

> Hey, sorry I've been neglecting you. Stuff got a bit complicated. I'm away now – home for Xmas – but let's get together once I'm back, yeah?

Ten days ago, this message would have made my day, but now it leaves me cold. I misjudged Riley. I thought he was an Aussie version of Shay Fletcher, cute and kind and cool, but it turns out he was just another dishwater boy, his

191

messages veering erratically between flirty and malevolent. I click Delete and the message vanishes.

My sisters have posted pictures on my SpiderWeb wall – a photo of the Christmas tree with Mum's vintage-style fairy on top from Skye; the still-empty stockings along the mantlepiece from Summer; a picture of Caramel the pony with mistletoe behind her ear from Coco. Even Cherry has posted a photo, a shot of the mirror above the fireplace, draped with greenery and fir cones. *Miss you, Honey xxx* is scrawled on the glass in lipstick.

I love that they've thought of me, posted pictures to wish me Happy Christmas even though it's still Christmas Eve back home. I wonder if there is frost on the grass, snow-flakes falling from a velvet sky? Here, the heat is already curling around me like an unwanted blanket, sticky, stifling.

I message back, then shower and dress. Dad gave me money to buy myself something for Christmas to go with the laptop; I went shopping with Emma and picked out a new dress and some art materials. I take out my new sketch-book and paints, position myself in front of the mirror and begin a self-portrait. A ghost girl takes shape on the paper, jigsaw pieces missing from her face, her body. She looks as if she might fall to pieces, but her eyes are bright and proud.

'Honey! Breakfast!'

Emma appears in the doorway, and I tidy up my things and go through to the kitchen. Dad is wearing a Santa hat and PJ trousers, making smoked salmon bagels. 'Happy Christmas, Princess!' he declares, pulling me in for a hug.

'Happy Christmas, Dad. Happy Christmas, Emma!' I say. I hand over presents, a DVD box set of a crime series Dad likes and a gift box of pamper goodies in her favourite fragrance for Emma. What with my laptop, dress and the art materials, Dad and Emma have been more than generous, but I'd give anything for a stocking filled with chocolate coins and tangerines and stripy socks, like the ones we have at Tanglewood. Christmas at Dad's house is very calm and grown-up.

I open my presents from Tara and Bennie, a cute notebook and a purse in the shape of an owl; they're the kind of things I'd have picked out back when I was twelve, but I'm stupidly touched. It's a long time since I've had friends who gave me cute presents instead of cigarettes and cider and invitations to all-night parties.

The phone rings and I swoop on it, hoping it's Mum or

my sisters, but all is silent as I hold the handset. 'Hello? Who's calling?' I ask. 'Coco? Is that you? Stop messing around!'

The line clicks and goes dead.

'Who was that?' Emma wants to know.

'It just went dead,' I shrug. 'I thought it might be Mum, but it couldn't have been. She said they'd Skype me tonight, at eight o'clock our time – they'll be asleep now.'

'Just a wrong number,' Dad says.

Emma's lips press into a tight line. 'On Christmas Day!' she says. 'Of all days!'

I frown, aware that Emma is unsettled by the call too. Later, she and I are getting the picnic ready, packing cold meats and tubs of salad from the deli. Emma slides champagne and orange juice into the cool bag, wedging them in with ice packs, balancing the box holding pavlova with strawberries and fresh cream on top. The mince pies are long gone, but I finished off the Christmas cake yesterday, cloaking it in golden marzipan and thick white icing that stands up in peaks the way Mum showed me. I wrap some slices in tinfoil for the picnic basket.

'See if your dad's ready, will you, love?' Emma says.

✿✿✿✿✿✿✿✿✿✿✿✿✿✿✿✿✿✿✿✿✿✿✿✿

I drift across to the open door. Dad is outside, by the pool, pacing and talking on his mobile. I tilt my head to one side, straining to catch the words.

'I know, I know,' he says, his voice low. 'It's hard for me too. But I've told you before not to call the house phone! What are you trying to do?'

My heart thumps, and unease prickles my skin like sweat. I step back into the cool of the house, smiling brightly at Emma. 'He's coming,' I tell her. 'Any minute.'

We drive to the beach, one of the busier ones along the coast from Sunset. Christmas lights have been strung along the dunes and a sound system is playing Christmas songs through huge speakers. A giant Christmas tree stands to one side of a festival-style stage, a blackboard advertising the bands playing later.

The beach itself is a patchwork of family picnics, random mini Christmas trees dotted here and there across the sand, the smell of dozens of disposable beach barbies gently charring Christmas dinner. I spot a group of girls my age playing volleyball in red bikinis with white funfur trim, older kids down by the water with surfboards. Everyone is wearing red hats, fake beards, antlers, tinsel.

❀❀❀❀❀❀❀❀❀❀❀❀❀❀❀❀❀❀❀❀❀❀❀❀

'Isn't it amazing?' Emma breathes. 'I knew you'd love it, Honey. It's so alive, so different!'

'Amazing,' I echo.

It really is. Not so long ago I'd have loved the bright, brash spectacle of it all. I'd have asked the bikini girls if I could join in with the volleyball game, wandered down to chat to the surfers, stayed out late to watch the bands and found a party to take me through till Boxing Day. Now, though, I am hiding behind sunshades and a floppy hat, smiling an empty smile. I feel hollow, like I left an important part of me behind at Heathrow Airport and haven't quite noticed until now.

I eat and laugh and say all the right things; I slather on suncream and stretch out in the sand, drink cold champagne mixed with orange juice. Nobody touches my home-made Christmas cake, and when I taste a piece it turns out to be cloying and heavy, too rich, too solid. I abandon the cake on its bright plastic plate and the sun dries it to a rubble of tasteless crumbs.

Eventually, bored and boiled alive, I head for the ocean, swimming up and down dutifully between the green flags until my limbs ache. Wading ashore, I realize I'm miles from where I started.

As I cross the crowded beach towards Dad and Emma, a couple of lads walk past with surfboards, laughing, talking, feet crusted with sand. A third boy follows, blond, tanned, wholesome, handsome; the last boy on earth I want to see right now. My heart flips over. He catches my eye and his face registers surprise, confusion.

Riley is just as gorgeous as I remember.

'Hey,' I say, keeping my voice steady. 'Thought you'd gone home for Christmas?'

'Home?' he echoes. 'I am home. I live in Sydney, born and bred. We've met before, yeah? Sorry . . . I can't quite remember your name. Remind me?'

I roll my eyes. Riley likes to play games, I know, but this one is ridiculous.

'It's Honey,' I say as brightly as I can. 'We met in November, at Sunset Beach. You rescued my sketchbook.'

'That's it!' he says, his face lighting up. 'I asked you to a party and you gave me the flick. Which is just as well because you're, what, like, fourteen or something?'

'Fifteen,' I say. 'And it can't have bothered you that much, or you wouldn't have added me on SpiderWeb.'

Riley frowns. 'OK,' he says. 'That's your British sarcasm

197

in action, right? I never quite got around to adding you on SpiderWeb. Sorry for that.'

I shiver, in spite of the scalding heat. Either Riley is a great actor or he's telling the truth, and much as I hate to admit it, I don't think he's faking the boredom and indifference as his eyes slide away from me and over to his mates.

'So. Happy Christmas and stuff,' he says. 'Nice to see you again, um . . . Honey? Gotta run.' He lopes across the sand towards his mates.

As far as I can tell, the boy I've just been talking to is not the boy who sent me flirty messages at 5 a.m., day after day for weeks on end. And if Riley isn't Surfie16 . . . then who is?

We leave the beach late afternoon, before the live music begins, and I don't even care. Dad and Emma are off to a client's cocktail party; Dad says it will probably be stiff and formal and achingly dull. I take the hint and wriggle out of the invite, but Emma isn't comfortable leaving me behind.

'Sure you won't come?' she asks, elegant in a chiffon dress, gold-hoop earrings reminding me yet again that my

❀❀❀❀❀❀❀❀❀❀❀❀❀❀❀❀❀❀❀❀❀❀

dad is not as perfect as I thought he was. 'It feels wrong, leaving you home alone on Christmas night.'

'We've been through all this,' Dad says. 'She'll be fine!'

'I really will,' I promise. 'Mum's Skyping at eight. I can't miss that!'

Dad tells me to say Happy Christmas to my sisters, and when I ask if he wants to hang on for half an hour and say it himself he looks at me like I am crazy.

'We can't be late,' he argues. 'It'd be incredibly rude, and Nielson's a guy I want to keep sweet. He could put a lot of work our way in the New Year.'

Is Dad serious? Work comes before family, even on Christmas Day?

Before I can argue, he swoops in to drop a swift kiss on my hair and steers Emma out to the car. I resist the impulse to throw the rest of the Christmas cake at the back of his head, but only just. That cake is solid – it could do a lot of damage.

As soon as I'm alone, I open my laptop and click on to SpiderWeb. Looking back over Surfie16's posts, I see how vague he has been each time I've asked about uni or where he lives; how he changed the subject if I mentioned the day we met. I wanted him to be Riley, and he played along – but Surfie16 could actually be anyone; his home page gives nothing away. He could be some middle-aged sicko who gets his kicks from flirting with young girls. The thought makes my skin crawl. And then I remember that I asked him to my house, gave him my address and mobile number.

Nausea rolls through me in waves, threatening to sweep me away.

I go to my friends' list, select his name and press Delete. Relief replaces the sick feeling. I have had a lucky escape, and I've learnt my lesson; I'll never take risks with Internet safety again.

Minutes later, the familiar jangly call-tone of Skype starts up. When I see Mum, Summer, Skye, Coco, Cherry and even Paddy jostling in front of the webcam all the bad stuff melts away and it is finally, finally Christmas. I watch as they open the presents I've sent them, then it's my turn to open my gifts from home. There's a cute boho slip-dress, a jewellery-making kit, a hairslide adorned with feathers. Here too, at last, are the silly little surprises that make Christmas magic back home: a snow globe, chocolate-flavoured lipgloss, a book by my favourite YA author and

❁❁❁❁❁❁❁❁❁❁❁❁❁❁❁❁❁❁❁❁❁❁❁

a fortune-telling fish that curls up on my palm to predict 'true love'. Yeah, right.

We talk for an hour, until Mum and Paddy have to go to finish off the cooking, and Coco finally asks about Dad. I tell her he's gone out, that he said to say Happy Christmas. 'He did send presents, didn't he?' I check.

'Money,' Summer tells me.

'Did you find out who hacked your SpiderWeb?' Coco whispers.

'Not exactly, but it turned out my privacy settings were way off . . . and let's just say there were a few people on there who weren't exactly friends. It shouldn't happen again.'

When the call ends, I take a deep breath. I kept it together, just about. I didn't cry, I didn't fall to pieces, I didn't let on that Christmas dinner at the beach wasn't a patch on the fabulous, familiar chaos of Tanglewood. I didn't say that all I really wanted was to be there, with them.

I notice one last present, slightly squashed, hidden away behind the torn tissue-paper wrappings. A box of Paddy's chocolates, six Sweet Honey truffles that haven't travelled well, sticky, melted, messy, spoilt.

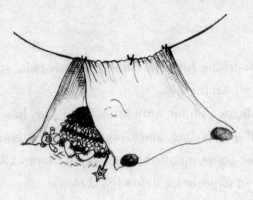

18

**Journal:
SweetHoney**

1 January, 4 a.m.
I resolve to start a SpiderWeb journal (starting now!)
I resolve to make the most of life in Australia
I resolve to get fit; get tanned; stop being homesick
I resolve to paint more
I resolve to have more fun
I resolve to stop waking at 4 a.m.

Last night was New Year's Eve, and I went out with Dad
and Emma. We went to a posh restaurant, then on to a
party on a boat thrown by yet another of Dad's business
contacts. The boat chugged its way round and round the
harbour while everyone partied; it would have been cool

if I hadn't been the youngest person there by a decade or so. At midnight the sky lit up with the best fireworks I've ever seen, and some old bloke with a comb-over tried to kiss me but I ducked out of the way at the last moment and locked myself in the ladies' toilet.

Today, I've been working on my art project. A few days ago I asked Mum to dig out a whole bunch of family photographs, school reports and letters, then scan and email them over. I've spent days turning them into collages and painting self-portraits over the top; in the images I look like I am wearing the past just beneath my skin.

My resolution to start writing in my SpiderWeb journal is linked to that – the project has got me thinking more about the past and the future, and writing stuff down might just help me sort out my messed-up head. I won't be sharing my diary entries with anyone, of course . . . I double-check to make sure the privacy settings are in place.

I rang home briefly from the boat party last night, but now Happy New Year messages begin to appear on my mobile as midnight strikes back home in Britain. One

❀❀❀❀❀❀❀❀❀❀❀❀❀❀❀❀❀❀❀❀❀❀❀

message comes from much closer, and makes my heart sink.

> Change of plan – my gran's had a fall and broken her ankle, so Mum and I are heading to Tas to help out for a couple of weeks. First Tara wimps out, now me . . . really sorry, Honey. Was so looking forward to the holidays too. We'll definitely be back the weekend before term starts. Let's do a sleepover and catch up on all the gossip, OK? Bennie x

Without Tara or Bennie around, the holidays no longer feel like fun – especially since Ash seems to have disappeared on me too. Who will I hang out with now? January stretches ahead like a blank page with the paint just out of reach. It feels empty, barren, a missed opportunity. I don't want to be stuck at the bungalow, watching DVDs with Emma and listening to the hushed rows that follow every time Dad stays out late.

Today, Dad and Emma sleep in for hours, and once they do surface it's clear they won't get any further than the sunloungers beside the pool. I pack away my art materials and take a walk down to Sunset Beach in the hope that this time, Ash *will* be there.

Thankfully, I see him as I walk in, whizzing up smoothies behind the counter, whistling while he works. He looks up and waves, his face creasing into a grin.

'Hey!' he calls. 'Where've you been? Thought you'd abandoned me!'

'Christmas,' I say with a shrug. 'And New Year, and all the madness in between. I did pop by a couple of times, but you weren't here.'

'Holiday hours,' Ash says. 'Everything's upside down. We've taken on extra staff, but today's guy hasn't turned up. Don't suppose you're any good with a tray?'

I laugh. 'I'm the best,' I tell him. 'You'd better believe it.'

After Dad left, Mum turned Tanglewood into a B&B and we all learnt how to wait tables and carry a loaded breakfast tray. It was never my favourite job, but I don't mind helping when I have to. I grab an apron from behind the counter, find the spray-cleaner and cloth, pick up a tray and head out to start clearing tables. Like I told Ash, I'm good. I know how to chat and schmooze the customers while I work, making old ladies smile, making little kids laugh, squeezing a last-minute tip from harassed mums and dads.

I am enjoying it so much I don't notice the time slide past; I clean and wipe and clear dirty dishes, stack the dishwasher and head out to clear tables again. By the time it's all under control, two new workers have arrived to take the evening shift and I seem to have landed myself a part-time job because one of them happens to be the manageress.

'Just temporary, mind,' she tells me. She's a sinewy, darkly tanned woman with a ponytail of multicoloured dreadlocks and a pierced nose. 'We've been left in the lurch and we do need someone . . . someone who's not scared of hard work. I've been watching you, and I think you're a natural.'

In the absence of anything more thrilling to do with my summer holiday, I take all of ten seconds to weigh up the offer. 'OK,' I say. 'Why not?'

Why not indeed? I asked for more fun in the New Year, and a job at the beach cafe could be the answer. It's a great way to meet new people and earn some pocket money too.

Ash hangs up his apron and the two of us walk down to the water's edge. 'It was a bit manic there for a while,' he says. 'Thanks for the help.'

❀❀❀❀❀❀❀❀❀❀❀❀❀❀❀❀❀❀❀❀❀❀❀

'No worries,' I reply. 'It was fun. And now it looks like you're stuck with me.'

'I like being stuck with you,' he says. 'We'll make a great team – it's going to be cool. So . . . how was your Christmas and New Year?'

I frown. 'It was OK. But Christmas on the beach? Just weird . . .'

I consider telling him about seeing Riley and how he wasn't on my SpiderWeb page after all, but the story is sad and twisted and I want to forget it ever happened.

'Maybe it's just because my mum and my sisters are so far away,' I conclude. 'I felt a bit homesick. I miss them.'

Ash laughs. 'Wish I could escape my lot sometimes,' he says. 'I think that's why I like the beach cafe – I get to be off-duty for a bit. I'm babysitting now. You'd be really welcome to come along and help . . . meet everyone . . . if you want to?'

'Babysitting?' I repeat. 'Seriously?'

'I'll throw in a free dinner if that'll swing it,' he says. 'Come on. My family – guaranteed to cure you of all home-sickness. Ten minutes with them and you'll want to be a hermit for the rest of your life.'

❀❀❀❀❀❀❀❀❀❀❀❀❀❀❀❀❀❀❀❀❀

'OK then!'

We turn away from the ocean and pick our way across the beach, through the wide streets that head up to Willow-bank and onwards along narrower, less leafy ones. The houses are smaller now; there are no gardens with swimming pools, no silver cars with retractable sunroofs.

'I think I told you I live with my sister and her family,' Ash says as we walk. 'Dad went back to Sri Lanka when I was born – he's been out of the picture so long it's as if he was never there to start with. And then . . . well, Mum died when I was twelve. My sister Tilani had just got married; she took me in, looked after me.'

My eyes widen. How many times have I moaned to Ash about broken families, how painful it was to choose between Mum and Dad, how annoying to have to put up with Paddy and Cherry? He never had that choice to begin with.

'Ash,' I whisper. 'I'm so sorry, I had no idea.'

'Long time ago now,' he says briskly. 'It's just the way things are. And it's why I try to babysit when I can, y'know? Make myself useful. So . . . here we are. This is home.'

Ash's house is a bungalow with a small yard to one side, a frazzled tree standing guard over a mess of toy trucks

and scooters and abandoned dolls. The French windows
are open and a cacophony of yelling, screeching and singing can be heard above the sound of the radio. He goes
inside.

'Hey, kids,' he says. 'I've brought a friend over.'

I step through the French windows and into chaos. Two
girls dressed in high-heeled shoes and curtain cloaks blink
at me, suddenly shy, while a boy wearing a cowboy hat and
a feather boa jumps forward, bringing a wooden sword
down in front of me.

'What's the password?' he demands.

'Caramelized kangaroo,' I say, not missing a beat.

'That's two words,' the boy tells me solemnly. 'It's actually just kangaroo.'

'Just testing,' I say, and he lifts the sword and grins at
me.

'These are my nieces and nephew,' Ash says. 'The beautiful princesses Dineshi and Sachi, and Ravi with the
sword . . .'

The eldest girl, who looks about six, swirls her curtain
cloak around her. 'We're playing make-believe,' she tells
me. 'D'you want to be a dragon or a princess?'

209

'She's a princess, silly,' the smaller girl says, slipping a hand into mine. 'A real one. Can't you tell?'

I feel my heart begin to melt, just a little, just round the edges. The kids are like smaller versions of Ash, with their nut-brown skin and blue-black hair and long-lashed, mocha-dark eyes. They could melt an iceberg, seriously.

By the time Ash's sister comes through from the kitchen, Dineshi and Sachi are dressing me in a plastic tiara and a silk dressing gown, while Ash gallops around on all fours with a tail made from a long green sock tucked into the waistband of his jeans. Tilani is a paramedic, like her husband, and is about to leave to start her shift.

'Sam will be home just after ten,' she tells us. 'Is that OK? I hope you can handle the chaos, Honey!'

'I am used to chaos,' I tell her. 'I have a big family too. It'll be fun!'

It is fun, too. After an hour of dressing-up games the kids collapse on beanbags, quizzing me about my life as a real princess and how I flew here across many oceans from a kingdom far, far away. Then Ash makes macaroni cheese for tea and I fashion a backyard tent by pegging bedsheets to the washing line, and we huddle inside as the sun goes down and eat by torchlight, picnic style. Eventually all three kids are in bed, only half washed, the girls still wearing tiaras and Ravi still clutching his sword. They lean against Ash as he reads fairy stories and make me promise to come again soon, not to fly away home.

'I won't disappear,' I promise.

When Sam gets back from his shift, Ash walks me home. We leave behind the shabby streets and crowded houses and he slips his hand into mine and holds on, tight, as if I really am a fairy-tale princess who might fly away at any moment.

In the end, my summer holiday scores low on wild beach parties and late nights. It scores high on princesses, dragons, wiping tables and serving smoothies; there's a fair bit of art project here and there too, although maths and French have fizzled a bit. It also scores high on hanging out with Ash, talking with Ash, walking home with Ash under the stars. I think I am starting to fall for him, and I guess I'd score that very highly indeed.

19

Tara is back from the Gold Coast now and Bennie's home from Tasmania, and it's my turn to host a sleepover. Emma is thrilled to be a part of it; she helps me plan a pool party and barbie with fresh fruit mocktails, and offers a selection of her favourite nineties teen flicks for us to watch. Dad is less enthusiastic.

'Why do they have to come here?' he grumbles. 'I don't get much time off. I certainly don't want to share it with a gaggle of silly girls!'

'It's Tara and Bennie,' I remind him. 'My best friends! They really want to meet you!'

'It's only one night, Greg,' Emma chips in. 'Honey hasn't had any friends over here before. It's not a lot to ask.'

'Why don't we go out?' he suggests. 'Leave them to it?'

'No, Greg, I want to do this properly,' Emma argues. 'We're responsible for other people's kids here. We need to be on the premises. We don't need to do anything – just stay in the background, help with the barbie. They'll be no trouble.'

'Please, Dad?' I chime in.

He rolls his eyes and ruffles my hair. 'Sheesh. I suppose so,' he sulks. 'Just this once, though, Honey. The next time you're inviting half the school over, ask first. I'll make sure I'm out of town!'

It bothers me that Dad can't make an effort for my friends, just like it bothered me that he wouldn't Skype my sisters on Christmas Day. But on Saturday afternoon when Dad tells Emma she's forgotten the most important ingredients for a sleepover – ice cream and popcorn – I hug him and tell him he's the best dad in the world for thinking of that.

'I'll sort it,' he says, grinning as he drives away. 'Won't be long!'

I don't worry, even when he's been gone for an hour. I don't worry when Tara and Bennie arrive and he's still not back, or when Emma texts and frowns and says that his mobile is off. I guess he's gone for a coffee or called into the office, found some time-wasting task to help him spin out the ice-cream expedition for a little while.

Or a long while.

'Is your dad around?' Tara asks.

'He will be,' I say. 'He's just nipped out to get ice cream and popcorn. He'll be back soon!'

'He is the best dad ever,' Bennie declares. 'My dad would never go to all that trouble!'

'Yeah,' I grin. 'He's cool!'

It's weeks since I've seen Tara and Bennie, and they've grown up a little. Bennie has taught herself to do cat's-eye eyeliner, and she's wearing a fifties-style swimsuit that's very Marilyn Monroe. She tells us about the boy she met in Tas who showed her that not all kisses are like cold dishwater soup.

We float on lilos in the pool, trailing our fingers in the water.

'I wish we had our own pool at home,' Tara sighs. 'You're sooo lucky!'

I already know that Tara's been texting the bus-stop boy all holidays, and that she thinks he might finally ask her out when the new term starts.

✿✿✿✿✿✿✿✿✿✿✿✿✿✿✿✿✿✿✿✿✿✿✿

'How about you?' Bennie asks, flicking a spray of water in my direction. 'Any hot romance? Did Riley ever surface again?'

'Did he ever,' I say. I've kept my Christmas Day encounter quiet, but now that I'm getting close to Ash it doesn't seem so sad, so scary any more.

'I saw him on Christmas Day, at the beach,' I confess. 'He barely recognized me. He was nice enough, but he wasn't interested . . . looks like the age difference really was a big issue for him.'

Tara frowns. 'So how come he added you on SpiderWeb then?'

'He didn't,' I say. 'Turns out that Surfie16 was just some random who added me. I assumed he was Riley and he just went along with it. Creepy, huh?'

'I *knew* something wasn't right about him!' Bennie declares. 'That's scary. I mean, you asked him round to your house, Honey! What if he'd turned up? And . . . well . . . he could have been an axe murderer or something!'

'He wasn't,' I say. 'And I've deleted him, anyway. Lesson learnt.'

❀❀❀❀❀❀❀❀❀❀❀❀❀❀❀❀❀❀❀❀❀❀

I let myself slide off the lilo and into the water, enjoying the cool.

'Report him,' Tara is saying. 'People can't just go around pretending to be other people on the Internet!'

'It's all over,' I say. 'No harm done. Anyway, that's not the big news. I didn't want to tell you by text or on Spider-Web, but I got myself a holiday job at the cafe. I've been seeing a lot of Ash . . .'

'You do fancy him!' Bennie whoops. 'What did I say?'

'I know, I know,' I laugh. 'Don't get too excited, though – it's early days. We're still at the hand-holding stage.'

'No kisses?' Tara asks, disappointed.

'We're taking it slow . . .'

As I say this, I realize that normally I jump headlong into relationships with all guns blazing; then again, I've never met anyone quite like Ash. I'm used to being in control with boys, calling the shots, but with Ash I am way out of my depth. I care about him so much it scares me. When he walks me home at night we hold hands, but what if it's normal for friends in Australia to hold hands? What if he doesn't actually fancy me at all?

I close my eyes and think about Ash; dark eyes fringed

216

with long lashes, sharp cheekbones, the sleek fall of his blue-black hair. I think about kissing him too; I think about that a lot.

I duck under the water and swim towards my friends, shark-like. I surface suddenly, tipping up the lilos and dragging Tara and Bennie into the water with much screeching, splashing and laughter. Heart-to-hearts are forgotten as we shower, change and fire up the barbie.

'I don't know where Greg can have got to,' Emma frets, checking her mobile for the hundredth time. 'I can't understand it!'

'Should we wait?' I ask.

'No, no, just go ahead, girls,' Emma says. 'Something must have come up. A call from the office . . .'

'On a Saturday?' Tara asks, frowning.

'He works long hours,' I explain. 'And there's a rush job on at the moment, so . . .'

'OK. Right,' Bennie says.

I turn away so they can't see my embarrassment.

We eat vegetable kebabs and baked bananas with melted chocolate as the sun sets. There is no ice cream and no popcorn, but nobody complains and eventually we retreat inside, where Emma has set out jugs of fruit juice and syrup and lemonade and soda, so that we can invent our own fancy mocktails. My friends like Emma – she's chatty and fun, and although at one point I panic that she might come through and watch *Clueless* with us, she just smiles and settles herself on the sofa with a glass of wine and tells us to have fun and not to stay up too late.

'Your stepmum's OK,' Bennie says, twirling the paper parasol in her drink as we curl up to watch the DVD.

'She's not my stepmum,' I correct. 'Just Dad's girlfriend. But yeah, she's OK. I'm sorry about Dad. I bet he popped into the office and got side-tracked . . . he's kind of a work-aholic. He probably forgot he'd promised ice cream.'

'It's no biggie,' Bennie shrugs. 'Mocktails are better!'

'Dads,' Tara agrees. 'What are they like?'

My friends are sleeping by the time Dad finally gets home in the early hours, but I am wide awake. I hear the low hiss of voices, the sound of Emma crying again, and I know for sure that I have heard it all before, over and over, right through my childhood. It's all too familiar, although I've never been able to admit it before.

I blotted out the rows, the arguments, told myself they

✿✿✿✿✿✿✿✿✿✿✿✿✿✿✿✿✿✿✿✿

were nightmares, whitewashed my memories so that every-thing looked perfect. I remember now, though, and my eyes sting with tears the way they did years ago when I used to sit at the top of the stairs late at night, hugging my knees, listening. It scared me then and it still scares me now, the sound of my dad when he's angry.

I open up my laptop and click on to SpiderWeb. I find a recent photo of me and Ash, our faces squashed up close, laughing into my iPhone camera with the ocean behind us, and post it on to my page. *Summer holidays so cool*, I type. *Wish they didn't have to end . . .*

Then I click to open the journal page to distract myself, writing through the night while my friends sleep on.

 **Journal:**
SweetHoney

28 January, 4.20 a.m.
Sleepover – that's a joke. I can't sleep . . . I may never sleep again.

My friends don't have that problem. Bennie is snoring slightly and Tara is wearing a kitten-print nightie that she's probably had since she was seven. My friends are not cool. Tara has a million freckles and geeky specs and zero dress sense. Bennie is one of those curvy girls that just miss out on that whole hourglass figure thing and end up looking like your favourite teddy bear. Still, at Willowbank they are practically fashionistas. That place is so stuck in the Dark Ages they will be adding kirtles, hoods and goatskin capes to the school uniform list any minute now. The place is so dull it makes my brain ache.

I don't think I'd survive it at all without Tara and Bennie. They are the sweetest, kindest girls I've met in forever. When we hang out I feel like I'm five years old again, in a good way. I feel happy and hopeful, like the world is a good place to be. And that's quite an achievement right now because my life is actually one big mess. It's a very long time since I've had proper friends, and boy, does it feel good. Hope to goodness I don't mess it up.

20

On Monday, I have to drag myself to school. It is an effort to pull on the blue-checked tent dress, an effort to pack my rucksack with books and study sheets and shiny new pencil case. The study timetable on the wall above my bed is looking neglected. I stopped sticking to the plan around the time I began working at the cafe; I haven't opened a maths book in weeks.

I meet Tara and Bennie in the foyer, and together we sit through an hour-long assembly where Miss Bird attempts to shake us out of our back-to-school gloom and instil a little enthusiasm for the year ahead. I close my eyes and doze through most of this speech, so I cannot tell whether it is successful or not.

My enthusiasm is at an all-time low. I slouch through

school, just waiting for trouble to find me. It will. Any initial veneer of being different, cool, exotic, are long gone, and hostile glances follow me along the corridors. The dodgy SpiderWeb picture from last term lost me a lot of friends, and my upbeat picture of me and Ash doesn't seem to have changed that. The fact is, I don't fit in – I must have been crazy to imagine I ever could.

It was fun to pretend for a little while. I tried, I really did, but the novelty has worn off and my acting skills won't keep me afloat for long once the teachers suss how little study I've actually done these last few weeks. I don't even have a visit to the beach cafe to look forward to – Ash isn't working today, and my part-time job is over now that the holiday rush is dying down. I am surplus to requirements.

Back home, I lean against the honeysuckle arch with a few maths books at my side, trying to recover some of the focus I had before Christmas. I am still frowning at the first problem when my mobile rings, Bennie's name flashing up.

'Hey, Bennie,' I say. 'Couldn't live without me for even half an hour, huh? I'm glad you called, though, because I'm totally stuck on my maths. That first question is a killer. Any clues?'

❀❀❀❀❀❀❀❀❀❀❀❀❀❀❀❀❀❀❀❀❀❀❀

There's a silence on the line, and a pink and white honeysuckle flower drifts gently down on to my work-sheet.

'Bennie?' I repeat. 'What's up?'

There's a snuffling sound at the end of the line, and then Bennie's voice comes through. 'You know what's up,' she says. 'You know exactly what's up, and that's fine, you're entitled to your opinion. I'm not going to argue. If you don't want our friendship, then fine –'

'Huh?' I cut in. 'What are you talking about? Of course I want your friendship!'

'You have a funny way of showing it,' she replies. 'You could have just said those things to our faces, Honey. You didn't have to humiliate us like that in front of everyone. Tara is gutted; I am too. Boy, did we get you wrong. We liked you. We *trusted* you!'

'Bennie!' I argue. 'Listen! Calm down, please. I have no idea what you are talking about! I think there's been some mistake –'

'No mistake,' Bennie says. 'Check your SpiderWeb, seeing as your memory's so poor today. And goodbye . . . been nice knowing you.'

❀❀❀❀❀❀❀❀❀❀❀❀❀❀❀❀❀❀❀❀❀❀

'Bennie!' I yell. 'Wait! Listen to me – whatever you've seen –'

But the line is dead. I jump up and run into my bedroom, open up my laptop and click through to my SpiderWeb page. I go cold all over.

A screenshot from my private SpiderWeb journal is posted up on the wall, part of the piece I wrote at the sleepover in the early hours of Sunday morning.

> Bennie is snoring slightly and Tara is wearing a kitten-print nightie that she's probably had since she was seven. My friends are not cool. Tara has a million freckles and geeky specs and zero dress sense. Bennie is one of those curvy girls that just miss out on that whole hourglass figure thing and end up looking like your favourite teddy bear. Still, at Willowbank they are practically fashionistas. That place is so stuck in the Dark Ages they will be adding kirtles, hoods and goatskin capes to the school uniform list any minute now. The place is so dull it makes my brain ache.

They are my words, my views, but taken out of context they look spiteful, bitchy. That's not how they were intended. That diary entry was about how much I love my friends, not how hopeless they are.

❀❀❀❀❀❀❀❀❀❀❀❀❀❀❀❀❀❀❀❀

That journal is supposed to be private – so how come it's plastered all over my home page? I look closer and see that both Bennie and Tara are tagged in the status, and that SpiderWeb says I posted it. But I didn't. I haven't touched my laptop since yesterday, and the status was posted a few hours back when I was still in school.

I scroll down, reading through the comments from girls at school. They call me two-faced, vicious, manipulative, mean. I can't even blame them – this looks bad. Who would do something like this – and how?

I click the Delete button, pick up my mobile and call Bennie and Tara over and over, but there's no reply. All I can do is post a status explaining that my page has been hacked, but when I go to check on it the words have vanished as if they were never there at all.

A new private message flashes up, and I go cold all over as I see the name: Surfie16.

> Don't hold back, Honey, will you? I know you said your new friends were kind of boring, but no need to broadcast it all over SpiderWeb. Harsh.

I take a deep breath.

❀❀❀❀❀❀❀❀❀❀❀❀❀❀❀❀❀❀❀❀❀❀

> Who are you? Leave me alone! I deleted you weeks ago, so why are you on my SpiderWeb page at all?

A reply pops up at once.

> You know exactly who I am – Riley. We met at the beach, right? You'll never delete me, Honey, you've been flirting with me from the start. You just can't stay away!

My hands are shaking as I type.

> I definitely deleted you, creep. You're not Riley. I know you're not. So who the hell are you?

Almost a minute ticks by, and then the answer is there:

> Wouldn't you like to know?

School the next day is pure torture. I look for Bennie and Tara in the foyer before lessons, but they're not there, and when I ask if anyone's seen them my classmates turn away, freezing me out completely. In maths, Tara has moved seats. She won't look at me, and when I try to talk to her afterwards, Liane tells me to back off, that I've done

226

enough damage already. I stand alone at break, the dagger glares of the girls around me piercing my skin. It's almost the end of lunchtime before I manage to track Bennie and Tara down, sitting at a picnic table by the school sports field.

They get up to leave as I approach, but I grab on to Bennie's arm, distraught.

'You have to listen,' I plead. 'I can explain! I didn't post those things. My laptop's been hacked again or something. I'd never have posted that, you know I wouldn't!'

'You're saying you didn't write it?' Bennie challenges.

'I did – but not like that!' I argue. 'It was taken out of context! I said lots of nice things about you too; it wasn't meant to be mean –'

'Wasn't it?' Tara says. Her eyes are pink from crying and I feel so bad for making her feel that way.

'It was posted yesterday afternoon while I was still in school,' I say. 'Think about it – I couldn't have posted it, could I? It wasn't me, you have to believe me!'

Bennie shakes her head. 'You may not have had your laptop in school, but you had your iPhone,' she says. 'You could have posted it from that.'

'I didn't!' I protest. 'Someone's hacking my SpiderWeb page. Why won't you believe me? Maybe Surfie16 really is some kind of stalker – he messaged yesterday and it was like he was laughing at me!'

'I thought you deleted him?' Tara challenges.

'I did!'

'Yeah, right. You obviously didn't.'

The bell for afternoon lessons rings out and Bennie sighs. 'It's funny how these things keep happening to you,' she says. 'That photo before Christmas; now this. It looks bad, but somehow, you're still the victim. Well, my heart bleeds for you, Honey. Look . . . I don't want this conversation right now. I don't know what to believe any more.'

Tears sting my eyes as they walk away. Battling to keep my head high, I elbow my way through the crowded corridors, find the nearest toilets and lock myself in a cubicle. I sink down on to the toilet seat, dismayed. My fresh start, already a little rocky, has finally imploded, and worse, someone is hacking my SpiderWeb and stirring up a whole world of trouble.

Aren't they? After two nights of little or no sleep, I can't even think straight. I feel like I'm going mad. I press my cheek against the Formica partition, wishing I was a million miles from here. I sit that way for a long time, and then someone rattles the cubicle door and I jump up, panicked. What am I even doing? I am not the kind of girl to hide, to cry, to fall to bits in public. I square my shoulders, grab my bag and walk out of there, stalking along the corridor as the last lesson-change bell sounds. I put up a hand to wipe away my tears and it comes back streaked with black eyeliner.

'Honey? Are you all right?'

I push past Miss Bird and walk on out through the double doors, across the courtyard, on to the street; I can hear the head teacher calling after me, but I don't look back.

Honey
<honeyb@chocolatebox.co.uk>
✉

to: benniej@oznet.com
cc tarastar@messagebox.co.au

I didn't do it, I really didn't. Please believe me.
xxx

21

The beach cafe is busy, but Lola lets me sit at the counter even though she knows very well I should be in school. I've downed three Cokes by the time Ash turns up to start his shift, and I feel jittery and giggly like a hyperactive child. Injustice and anger slosh around inside me like poison.

'You should go home, Honey,' Lola says as she leaves. 'Chill. I know you're upset . . . but trust me, it'll all blow over. Whoever said schooldays are the best days of our lives was definitely having a laugh.' I drag up a smile and Lola hugs me quickly, hangs up her apron and hands the till key to Ash.

'What's up?' he asks me as soon as she's gone. 'How come you're here before me? How long *have* you actually been here?'

'Don't ask,' I tell him. 'Am I a bad person? A mad person? OK, so I probably shouldn't have written those things, but they were my private thoughts, right? They were never meant to be seen by anyone else!'

He frowns. 'Honey? Have you been crying?'

'No,' I growl. 'I never cry. It's just that my eyeliner smudged, OK?'

Ash takes my hands. 'Look, I know something's wrong,' he says. 'It's just that I have no clue what you're talking about –'

'Fine,' I bark, pulling away from him, stepping behind the counter and scanning the shelves. 'Is there any cider in that fridge?'

'You know there isn't.'

'God, you're so *boring*!' I huff. 'This whole place sucks! Doesn't anybody around here ever have any *fun*?'

'Look, Honey,' Ash says, trying to take my arm and steer me out from behind the counter. 'I don't know what's wrong but I know something is. Why don't you go home, like Lola said –'

I turn on him, blazing. 'Oh, sure, why don't I?' I snarl. 'That would be much more convenient. You'd be rid of me – you wouldn't have to worry about my car crash of a life. You wouldn't have to worry about anything. That's right, push me away, chuck me away, shove me in a corner out of sight so I'm somebody else's problem. That's OK. I'm used to it. It's been happening for years . . .'

The whole cafe is silent and staring, but I'm too angry now to care.

'I'm not pushing you away,' Ash says, exasperated. 'That's the last thing I'd do. If you don't want to go home, stay here with me. Sit up by the counter, talk to me –'

'Who says I want to talk to you?' I fling back. 'I don't. I don't want to talk to anyone – whatever I say will just get twisted anyhow. Everything's ruined. So hey, don't let me distract you from your job. You have a cafe to look after, and ice-cream sundaes are clearly more important than friends in trouble. Get lost, Ash!'

I turn on my heel and walk away, out of the cafe and along the beach, hands over my ears so I can't hear Ash's yells telling me to come back.

It takes about ten minutes' walking for me to calm down again, and by that time the beach cafe is just a dot in the distance behind me. I kick off my hated brown sandals, peel off the knee-high socks and abandon them on the sand so I can walk along the water's edge kicking at the surf.

I am an expert at toddler-style tantrums, drama-queen strops, but now I've cooled down I feel worse than ever. I went to the cafe to see Ash because I thought he was the one person who might just understand; instead of giving him a chance to do that, I yelled at him, flung every shred of kindness and sympathy back in his face.

What can I say? Today has been a losing friends kind of a day.

I am an expert at giving up, running away. Sometimes it feels like freedom, but today I know it's just defeat, pure and simple.

I leave Sunset Beach behind, clambering over rocks and following the tideline into another cove, less pretty, more shingly, almost deserted. My rucksack is annoyingly heavy; I ditch a maths book to make it lighter, then turf out my pencil case, my gym shoes, my French dictionary and finally the rucksack itself. I don't even care any more.

I spot a bonfire in the distance, up on the dunes, a bunch of backpackers gathered round it. The thin plume of smoke reminds me of Tanglewood, of hope. I pull off the yellow

❀❀❀❀❀❀❀❀❀❀❀❀❀❀❀❀❀❀❀❀

neckerchief and throw it into a rock pool, heading towards the sound of laughter, the smell of woodsmoke.

By the time Ash finds me there, two hours later, I am happy again. I am the life and soul of the party, dancing, flirting, smoking, drinking. My throat aches with the harsh burn of cigarettes; no amount of lager can wash the stale, sour taste away. Two or three of the boys are hanging on my every word, and that feels good. The backpackers are mostly from Britain and France, students on a gap year; soon they will be heading on again, some for Brisbane, some to New Zealand, some for Thailand. I am seriously considering tagging along.

When I see Ash walking towards me in the falling light, hope leaps inside me; then I see his face, grim, unsmiling. He walks up to me and takes the ciggy from my lips, grinding it into the sand with his heel, prising the can of lager from my fingers, throwing the contents across the dunes.

'Hey!' I yell, outraged. 'What are you doing? Leave me alone!'

'You'd like that, wouldn't you, Honey?' he growls. 'Then you could carry on with your little self-destruct jag without any hassles. OK, you're upset – but this isn't going to help!

As for you guys . . . what are you even doing giving her drinks and smokes? Are you crazy?'

My backpacker friends seem slightly bemused.

'Hey, hey,' one of them says, challenging Ash. 'What's it to you, anyway? Leave the girl alone!'

'She's just a kid,' Ash says. 'She's fifteen, OK?'

'Oh, great,' I snarl. 'Thanks for that, Ash. What does my age have to do with anything? And what does my life have to do with you anyhow? Get lost!'

'I won't,' Ash says. 'I care about you, OK? I've been worried sick!'

'Well, you can stop worrying,' I snap. 'I've had a change of plan. Australia's not working out for me, so I'm going to travel – Thailand . . . India . . . right?'

I look at my new friends for backup, but they are shrugging, turning away. Only one boy sticks up for me. Perhaps he's hoping that the lager and ciggies he's been feeding me for the past two hours might still buy him a moonlit snog on the dunes. It won't, though. Not now.

'You heard the lady,' he sneers at Ash. 'Back off!'

In the fading light he looks kind of seedy, sinister.

'Look, it's OK,' I say, defeated. 'Ash is a friend.'

❀❀❀❀❀❀❀❀❀❀❀❀❀❀❀❀❀❀❀❀❀

The backpacker boy rolls his eyes, disgusted.

Ash takes my hand and leads me away from the bonfire, and the fuzzy, light-headed bubble I've been hanging on to deflates abruptly like a burst balloon. Reality floods back. I insulted Ash, yelled at him, embarrassed him in front of a cafe full of customers. Yet the minute his shift was over he came looking for me. Clearly, he is the crazy one around here.

'How did you find me?' I ask as we trudge across the dunes. 'How did you know where I'd be?'

'You left a trail,' Ash says, holding up a bulging, dripping, sand-encrusted rucksack. 'Sandals, socks, books, neckerchief. It was like a treasure hunt, only without the nice surprise at the end. And I could only find one shoe . . .'

'Good,' I say. 'I hated them anyway.'

'Are you drunk?'

'No!' I say, outraged again. 'Of course I'm not! I only had one can.'

'You sound drunk,' he huffs. 'And you smell like an ashtray.'

I sit down on a rock, gloomy.

'What about the kids?' I ask. 'Aren't you babysitting today?'

'Supposed to be,' Ash says. 'I rang my sister, told her something came up. She said she'd get a neighbour to sit with them.'

I wasn't sure that anything could make me feel worse, but that does.

'See?' I say in a small voice. 'I'm trouble. I have seriously messed up. Someone posted a page from my online diary on to my SpiderWeb wall, and now Tara and Bennie aren't talking to me. Actually, nobody is talking to me. Nobody wants me – I'm useless, worthless, a walking disaster area. I told you before, everything I touch turns to dust.'

'You're touching me,' he points out, pressing his palm against mine. 'I'm still here, aren't I? You've yelled at me, sworn at me, pushed me away, but I'm still here.'

'I know,' I admit. 'That's the bit I can't work out.'

'Thing is, I can see you,' he says. 'I can see past the goody-two-shoes act, past the tough-girl act, the self-destruct act, the drama-queen act. You've got about a million masks, Honey Tanberry, but none of them work on me. I can see *you*. And I think you're brave and strong and lovely.'

A salty tear slides down my cheek and Ash wipes it away gently, leaning his forehead against mine. He is so close I

✿✿✿✿✿✿✿✿✿✿✿✿✿✿✿✿✿✿✿✿

can feel the warmth of his breath, the flutter of his lashes. My eyes close and I think the world might slide away as his lips touch mine, softly, slowly, carefully. My fingers trail against his skin, tracing his cheekbones, the faint sandpaper stubble of his chin. I want to hold on and never let go, but as unexpectedly as it began, the kiss is over.

You might think that only bad things, sad things, can hurt you, but you'd be wrong. Lovely things can hurt you more because they thaw out the bits of your heart that you thought would be frozen forever. I can't help wondering if it might not be safer to stay frozen.

The trouble is, I think it's too late.

Honey
<honeyb@chocolatebox.co.uk>

to: benniej@oznet.com
cc tarastar@messagebox.co.au

I guess you're still angry with me and I deserve it,
I know. I'm sorry. I miss you both so much. Please,
can we at least talk?
xxx

SweetHoney16

22

A kiss can't fix my messed-up life, sadly.

The next morning I wake as usual at 4 a.m., drifting out of a dream about Ash. Reality seeps in, and I remember yesterday in all its gory detail. I open up my laptop. There are four new private messages on SpiderWeb, and my heart lurches; they're not from Tara or Bennie, but the girls at school. I force myself to read:

> What is WRONG with you, Honey? Stay away from Tara and Bennie. With friends like you, who needs enemies?

> If you think Willowbank is such a dump, why don't you go back to England? We don't want you here.

Classy. I don't know how you behave back in Britain but here in Aus we don't stab our friends in the back. You have a lot to learn.

You really are a bitch, aren't you?

That last one makes me flinch. Is this what they're thinking behind the silence, the glares? I am used to being dramatic, rebellious, notorious even, but I am not used to being hated. Back home I had a bad reputation, sure, but I never knowingly hurt anyone. When the other kids looked at me there was admiration, awe even, in their eyes. It's only since I started to clean up my act that things have gone so badly downhill. Kind of ironic.

I cannot face school today; I don't think I can face it ever again. When I hear Dad and Emma get up I wander out into the kitchen, the sheet wrapped round me.

'I'm not well,' I whisper. 'My head's sore, I feel sick and I've hardly slept . . .'

Well, it's the truth.

'Two days back at school and you're taking a sickie already?' Dad begins, but Emma hushes him, putting her hand against my forehead.

❀❀❀❀❀❀❀❀❀❀❀❀❀❀❀❀❀❀❀❀❀❀

'No temperature,' she says. 'But one day off won't hurt, Greg. Stay in bed, Honey, snuggle up . . . you'll feel much better tomorrow.'

I seriously doubt it, but Emma promises to call the school and I am off the hook, for today at least. I go back to bed and pull the sheet over my head. One thought keeps running through my mind – how could a page from my private journal end up posted on my SpiderWeb wall? I check my page again and something new has appeared, a picture of an old suitcase covered in labels from around the world, apparently posted by me. The caption reads: *Australia sucks . . . won't miss it one bit.*

Underneath, the comments have already started.

Good riddance.

Yeah, we'll miss you too. Don't come back.

I click Delete, but the post reappears a minute later, right before my eyes, and that's seriously scary. Am I going crazy? Who would do something like this? Not Ash . . . I've seen for myself the ancient computer in the corner

❀❀❀❀❀❀❀❀❀❀❀❀❀❀❀❀❀❀❀❀❀

of his living room. Not Tara or Bennie . . . they've been around my laptop a couple of times, but they wouldn't have faked the shock and hurt of seeing that diary page. I can think of someone who might have, though – Surfie16.

He is not the person he says he is, and he seems to be enjoying my torment. I click through to his home page, but it gives nothing away. There is the familiar profile picture, a close-up of bare feet and the tip of a surfboard. There is the cover image, a cool Aussie beach. He has only six friends listed, and each has a generic profile picture: a can of beer, a map of Australia, a surfboard, a rock band CD cover. Some of them I recognize as people who've posted nasty comments on my page, and now I begin to wonder if they too are as fake as Surfie16.

It's as if this profile is just a way to access my SpiderWeb page and get at me. I go to my friends' list and delete him all over again, adding a 'block from page' sanction to make sure he can't do any more damage.

I pass the day making a frantic series of self-portraits. The girl in the pictures looks exhausted, as if she might unravel at any moment; it's exactly how I'm feeling.

❀❀❀❀❀❀❀❀❀❀❀❀❀❀❀❀❀❀❀❀❀

Emma comes back from work and offers me paracetamol, iced water, buttered toast and kindness, but none of those things can fix the mess I'm in. 'Greg's working late again,' she tells me. 'I have my Pilates class – he was going to pick me up from there, but I'm happy to cancel and stay home with you if you'd rather.'

I open my mouth to tell Emma what's going on in my life, but the words won't come. 'No, no, just go,' I say. 'No worries.'

I want her to turn round at the last minute and ask me what's wrong, to look at me and see that the problem is not a twenty-four-hour bug but something much more serious. She doesn't, of course.

Once I'm alone again, I check my SpiderWeb page; another picture has appeared, an old one where I'm sticking my tongue out at the camera. It was a joke, something Coco took on my phone one day last year, but out of context it just looks crazy, confrontational. As for the status I'm supposed to have written, it's vile.

Unbelievably, Surfie16 has made the first comment.

Nice. Showing your true colours, Honey.

❀❀❀❀❀❀❀❀❀❀❀❀❀❀❀❀❀❀❀❀❀

My hands shake as I hit Delete. How can this be happening?

Somewhere in the distance, the doorbell rings; I panic a little; the shrill ringing sound seems scary, threatening. When it rings a third time, I swear under my breath. 'OK, OK!' I yell. 'Wait a minute!'

Raking a hand through my tangled hair, I open the door a crack and there on the doorstep is Ash, with two small princesses and a dragon in tow.

The most amazing thing about small children is that they don't notice that you're wearing crumpled sleep shorts and a vest top with toast crumbs on the hem, or that your hair hasn't been combed, that your eyes are pink from crying and shadowed with lack of sleep. They just barge right in and hug you round the waist and jump up and down on your bed as if it's a trampoline.

Being caught looking like death by the boy who kissed you just yesterday afternoon is not so great. I pull on a kimono wrap and some sunshades to hide behind.

'Sorry,' Ash says, not looking sorry at all. 'The only way I could get out was to bring the whole tribe. Coming out to play?'

❀❀❀❀❀❀❀❀❀❀❀❀❀❀❀❀❀❀

'Can't,' I whisper. 'Not feeling so good, as you can see.'

'You look pretty awesome to me,' he says.

I smile. I look like death and I feel almost as bad, but Ash isn't judging me. He takes my hand and we sit side by side on the window sill as the kids explore the en-suite bathroom, switch the fairy lights on and off, hang bracelets from the dressing table over their ears.

'So,' Ash says quietly. 'You skipped school today.'

'Been ill,' I say with a shrug. 'As you can see. Some weird Aussie bug. Maybe I'm just allergic to the land of sunshine and opportunity? Besides, I only have one sandal.'

'You can't blame me for that,' he says. 'I did my best. It's probably floating along the coast of Papua New Guinea by now.'

I shrug. 'Can't say I miss it.'

The kids drift over to join us. 'Is your house a palace?' Sachi asks, eyes wide. 'How many mattresses have you got? Because a real princess needs ten or twenty, and even then she might not sleep at night if someone's put a pea underneath the bottom one. That's how you can tell if someone's really a princess.'

Ash laughs. 'You've been reading her too many fairy tales.'

'I don't sleep at night, now that you mention it,' I tell Sachi. 'I am nocturnal. Like an owl or a fox or . . . well, whatever you have over here. Only instead of flying around or rummaging through your dustbins, I paint pictures until the sun comes up.'

'You might need another mattress then,' Sachi says. 'Can we play dressing-up?'

After some frenzied ransacking of drawers and wardrobe, the girls gallop around in wedge sandals and bright skirts and scarves while Ravi performs a hip-swinging dance with a pair of my best polka-dot knickers on his head. It is the best distraction ever from being stalked by a mad Internet troll, trust me.

'Your friends came into the beach cafe asking after you,' Ash comments. 'Said you hadn't answered their texts or SpiderWeb messages.'

'Tara and Bennie? But . . . they haven't texted or messaged me!' I look at my iPhone for the hundredth time today; there are no messages at all.

'They have,' Ash says with a frown. 'They said you're

not answering, that you think somebody's messing with your SpiderWeb page.'

'Seriously? They believe me?' A flicker of hope stirs inside me.

'They're worried,' Ash says. 'I am too. If there's some Internet bullying thing going on, tell someone about it!'

'Who?' I fling back at him. 'Dad's never here, and Emma just brushes stuff under the carpet, pretends life is great. Well, it isn't. Look at me . . . I'm a wreck. Things keep popping up on SpiderWeb, stupid photos with nasty taglines that look like I've posted them when I really haven't. And there are all these hateful comments from kids at school, and some from strangers.'

Ash is on his feet, opening up my laptop, clicking on to the web browser.

'You leave yourself logged in all the time?' he asks as my SpiderWeb opens. 'That's crazy. Anybody could have got hold of this. If they can access your page, they can change the settings, post things in your name. Tara and Bennie said they definitely messaged you on here as well, so what if whoever is doing this is deleting stuff too?'

I bite my lip, leaning over his shoulder.

'Actually . . . I haven't had a message from home for days,' I say. 'Nothing from my mum or my sisters. That's a bit weird – if they'd seen the things on my home page they'd have been in touch, wouldn't they?'

'This is serious, Honey,' Ash says. 'I think you've been properly hacked. Someone's blocking your real friends and family as well as posting all this . . . this rubbish.' He scrolls down the page, disbelieving, and my cheeks flood with shame as he sees the pictures. How can anyone look at those images and not think badly of me?

I watch as he deletes the posts again and adjusts the privacy settings to maximum, but there's a feeling of dread inside me. Each time I delete something, the image comes back.

'Remember I told you that Riley added me on Spider-Web?' I ask. 'I used to chat to him online lots before Christmas, but it turns out it was never Riley at all – his username is Surfie16 and I think he might be the hacker. I keep deleting him, but he just comes back. Oh, Ash . . . I've been so stupid!'

He frowns. 'Look,' he says, 'if some creep has control of

your computer you need proper backup – tell your dad, OK? Promise?'

He shuts the laptop lid firmly. All three kids have stopped cavorting now and are staring at us, wide-eyed. 'Has somebody been mean to you, Honey?' Ravi asks. 'Shall I bring my sword next time?'

I dredge up a smile. 'It's nothing,' I say. 'Just silly people playing a silly practical joke. I'm fine, really.'

I break out a picnic supper of TimTams and orange juice and we sit out beside the honeysuckle arch as the light fades. The kids nag me for a story, and because there are no picture books at Dad's house I invent one, all about a princess who lives in a turret room. Her prince runs off with a wicked witch disguised as the princess's sister, so she chops off her beautiful hair and flies away to a land where everything is upside down and nobody is quite what they seem.

'It's not a very happy story,' Dineshi points out. 'How does it end?'

'I don't know, yet,' I admit.

'Do you need a prince to rescue you?' Ravi asks. 'I could

do it, when I'm not actually being a dragon. Or Ash could, maybe.'

I smile, and tell Ravi that princesses these days like to rescue themselves, but that it can take time to figure out who are the goodies and who are the baddies.

'We're the goodies,' Sachi says firmly, threading honeysuckle blossom into my hair like a crown. 'OK?'

It takes a while to wipe chocolate from mouths and remove random skirts and shawls and jewellery from the kids, but in the end my visitors are ready to head off. I try not to feel abandoned.

Ash leans over and kisses my cheek when the kids aren't looking, and I resist the temptation to grab on to him and never let go.

'Don't let this idiot hacker win,' he says. 'Tell your dad. Get some help. Then delete the whole account. That should do it.'

I'm glad I'm wearing sunshades. I wouldn't want him to see the tears in my eyes.

Summer Tanberry
<summerdaze@chocolatebox.co.uk>
to me ✉

Honey, I think there might be something wrong with
your SpiderWeb? I had a picture of the gypsy cara-
van with snow on it to post on your wall, but whenever
I try to post a warning comes up saying I've been
blocked. I know you wouldn't do that, but Coco and
Skye say it's happened to them too, so . . . I thought
I'd let you know. Plus, you're not answering my texts. I
expect that means you're too busy having a wild time
to talk to your little sisters, but hey.
Summer oxox

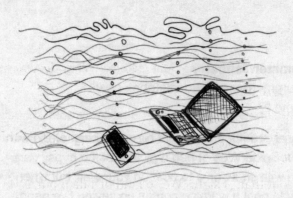

23

Asking for help has never been my strong point, but I know that if all of this was happening back home, I'd have told Mum by now. Mum's not here, but Dad and Emma are the next best thing. I pull the kimono wrap around me and slip into the living room just as they arrive home. It's not the best timing in the world, but I can't keep pretending that everything's OK – this SpiderWeb hate campaign is driving me crazy.

'Feeling better?' Dad asks as Emma pours him a glass of wine. 'It isn't good to give in to these things, Honey. This is an important year for you at school.'

I take a deep breath. 'I wanted to talk to you about that,' I say. 'I'm not sure I'm actually settling in at Willowbank. It's all gone a little bit wrong.'

Dad frowns. 'Wrong?' he echoes. 'What do you mean? Of course it hasn't!'

Emma pats my shoulder. 'You're doing fine!' she tells me. 'Lots of studying, lovely friends . . . Tara and Bennie are great!'

'About that,' I sigh. 'We've kind of fallen out.'

'I was always falling out with friends at school,' Emma says. 'It'll blow over!'

I bite my lip. Emma hasn't got a clue – this isn't a row about a borrowed eyeshadow or a copied homework; it's way more complicated than that.

'You're not listening,' I say. 'I'm in real trouble. Everything's gone wrong! Someone is posting really horrible stuff on my SpiderWeb page and half the school are chipping in with comments –'

Dad slams his glass down, spilling red wine on to the pale oak table.

'For goodness' sake, Honey!' he snaps. 'You're fifteen, not five! If you don't like the things people post online, stay off the Internet. As for school, no, it's not easy – get used to it! Sometimes in life you have to do things you're not keen on. Work hard, pass your exams, don't let a silly schoolgirl tiff derail you!'

❁❁❁❁❁❁❁❁❁❁❁❁❁❁❁❁❁❁❁❁❁❁❁

Tears sting my eyes, but I blink them back, defiant.

'Dad,' I whisper, 'you said that if Willowbank didn't work out I could try the other school. I just think –'

'That's enough!' Dad growls. 'Can't you see, Honey, there's a pattern in all of this? You're addicted to trouble. You like the fuss, you like the drama. Your mother's let you get away with murder. Well, not any more! You've been given a chance to start over – don't throw it all away!'

'Thanks, Dad,' I say. 'It's great to know you're always there for me.'

Dad's still yelling an answer to that as I run to my room and slam the door behind me. He may as well have slapped my face – he's told me flat out that he doesn't have time for my troubles. I love him more than anyone else in the world – you don't get to choose who you love – but I'm worn out with trying to make him love me back.

He left when I was twelve. I told myself it was a mistake, that he'd come back, but when he didn't, the hurt curdled into anger and I started smashing up everything I had left. I thought that if he could see how upset I was, he'd come back, reach out his arms and hold me tight, safe from all the chaos. When he moved to Australia it felt like the worst rejection ever; I thought that if I could somehow get there too, everything would be all right.

Well, I got to Australia, I got Dad's attention. I managed to keep it for two or three whole days, and then the novelty of having his long-lost daughter around wore off for Dad. I was just one more chore to take up his time, demanding, annoying, scrambling for the crumbs of his attention like a dog under the table. It's not as if it's any better for Emma – it doesn't take a genius to figure out that Dad's new happy family set-up is even shakier than the one he walked away from in Somerset.

I'm in trouble, real trouble, and my own dad does not want to know.

Next morning, I trick Emma into allowing me another day off school, pressing a hot flannel against my forehead to give the impression of a fever. Dad barely looks up as I trail across the kitchen to plead my case; if I fell down dead in the middle of the breakfast area I think he'd complain that I was cluttering the place up. Emma tells me they're meeting friends for dinner and will be back late, but to call if I need anything. Yeah, right.

❁❁❁❁❁❁❁❁❁❁❁❁❁❁❁❁❁❁❁❁❁❁

I prop the mirror on to my desk, ready to sketch out another self-portrait, but as I adjust the angle the mirror slips and falls down behind. When I move the desk to rescue it, I see that the mirror has cracked and shattered, like a jagged glass spider's web. Seven years' bad luck . . . that's all I need.

Peering into the broken mirror I see a scared, broken girl, her features sliced up into fragments. It's how I feel inside, how I've felt for a long time. I pick up a pencil and capture the image on paper, over and over. I try not to think about the laptop sitting in the corner of the room, it's green power-light taunting me. I don't want to look; I daren't, but it's all I can think about.

When I'm too tired to draw any more I hunt through the jewellery kit Mum bought me for Christmas, pulling out a card of thin silver wire, soft enough to cut with scissors, and a roll of see-through nylon line. Slowly, I prise chunks of broken glass away from the mirror, wrapping each one with a criss-cross of wire until thirty shards of mirror hang in the bedroom window; suspended on fishing line, spinning softly, catching the light like crystals.

I am aiming for a curtain effect, so that everything I see is shattered and spoilt. Instead, the shards snatch up rays

❀❀❀❀❀❀❀❀❀❀❀❀❀❀❀❀❀❀❀❀❀❀

of sunlight like a prism, sending dozens of tiny rainbows dancing all around me.

Finally, all out of distractions and willpower, I give in and check SpiderWeb. All of yesterday's deleted pictures are back. There's a new one too, a close-up, smiley photo of me that Emma took on the steps of the Sydney Opera House. It isn't sleazy, it isn't snarky – it's just ripped right down the middle and spattered with what looks like blood. I feel physically sick.

Surfie16 has already added a comment.

> Things not working out in Australia, Honey? Looks like you're finally losing it. Or is this just a clever way of telling us you're two-faced?

With fingers cut and bleeding from a dozen tiny glass cuts, I type out a message.

> Who are you? Why are you doing this?

Instinct tells me he's involved, and the reply confirms it.

> You'll find out soon enough.

❀❀❀❀❀❀❀❀❀❀❀❀❀❀❀❀❀❀❀❀❀❀❀❀

Fear slides down my spine like sweat. Remembering Ash's advice, I open up my SpiderWeb settings and click on Delete Account. Everything finally disappears, and the relief is instant, liberating. Why did I take so long to let go? I don't need SpiderWeb; for the last few days I've felt like a fly, trapped inside it, waiting to be picked apart by some invisible spider. The fallout from all of this will take some cleaning up, but at last the page has gone. The damage stops here.

Over on the bedside table, my iPhone bleeps and I open my text messages, looking for messages from Tara and Bennie. The screen flashes up an unknown number.

Nobody likes you, English girl. Nobody ever will.

I drop the phone on to the floor, my fingers shaking, but it bleeps again.

Worried yet? You should be. I'm watching you.

I go cold all over. I run to the window, but my bedroom looks out on to the garden; there is nobody there, nobody watching. It's just somebody trying to scare me, and doing a great job of it. It buzzes a third time.

> Don't believe me? You will. I know all about you . . . all the secrets you thought you'd left behind. And by the time I'm finished, everyone else will know them too.

Another text buzzes through, and I force myself to look, in spite of everything.

> Check your SpiderWeb . . .

I know I shouldn't; I know that I've deleted my page now, that the whole trolling thing should be over, even if the texting is not. Still, I find myself opening up my laptop, clicking on the bookmark to SpiderWeb.

And it's still there. Every hideous, leering photograph, every snarky, spiteful comment, all of it. Nausea rolls through my body in waves. I can't delete the posts and I can't deactivate the page . . . I can't do anything at all to stop it. Can I?

Slowly, the nausea turns to fury. I want to rewind, wipe out the last two months, erase this whole mess. Looking

❀❀❀❀❀❀❀❀❀❀❀❀❀❀❀❀❀❀❀❀❀

through the curtain of spinning glass shards, I see the swimming pool, glinting turquoise in the sun.

I run outside, carrying my laptop and iPhone, my bare feet burning on the hot flagstones, breathing in the scent of honeysuckle, heavy, intoxicating. One good throw is all it takes; I watch both iPhone and laptop sink down through the turquoise water, moving more slowly than you'd think. I'm looking for relief, rescue, but instead my eyes fill with tears; this won't change a thing because the hacker still has control of my SpiderWeb page. I'm trapped, helpless.

Crouched on the edge of the pool, I let myself fall forward, diving down to the bottom. I have some vague idea of rescuing the laptop, but of course, that would be pointless; it's wrecked now, ruined. It's funny how quiet it is underwater. Everything is slower, softer; the world seems muffled, far away. Of course, the minute I touch the blue tiles at the bottom I start to float up again, so, stubborn, I catch hold of the foot of the ladder and hold on. I want to prolong the moment, hang on to the feeling of peace. And then it becomes a challenge, a dare. My lungs burn and bubbles of air escape, rising up to the surface like a warning flare. My cut fingers are screaming with pain as the

✿✿✿✿✿✿✿✿✿✿✿✿✿✿✿✿✿✿✿✿✿✿✿

chlorine burns them, but my hands hold tight and my chest aches and my head fills up with darkness.

I take a great gulp in, swallowing water, and suddenly I am breaking the surface, lungs bursting, floundering for the side. I drag myself out of the pool and huddle on the grass, shaking, sucking in long, gasping breaths. I'm so shocked my mind can't make sense of anything, and shame and self-pity seep through my body like poison. I sit like that for a long time, until my breathing calms and my PJs have dried against my skin. After a little while the sun eases my shivers and I notice the deep blue sky, the golden sun, the scent of jasmine. I hear the flutter of parakeets darting between the trees like brief flashes of rainbow, and I stretch out under the honeysuckle and let myself fall into sleep.

When I wake, there are three figures crossing the driveway, two of them in familiar blue uniform. Tara, Bennie and Ash walk towards me across the grass, and for a moment I don't know whether to be happy or sad or scared or ashamed. Maybe there's a bit of all those things.

'Hey,' Ash says. 'Don't tell me. You decided to go for the

whole swim-in-your-clothes thing again. English girls . . . crazy!'

This is a little too close for comfort, and even Ash seems to know it. His soft brown eyes are dark with worry.

'I didn't do it,' I whisper as my friends kneel down on the grass beside me. 'Post that diary thing – I promise I didn't. I wrote it, but it was meant to be private; if you saw the whole thing you'd see that actually it was all about how much I cared –'

'We know,' Tara interrupts. 'We've been trying to tell you, but you haven't answered our texts or messages.'

'My iPhone's been hacked, blocked,' I say, eyes drifting towards the pool. 'And now it's broken. My laptop too . . .'

Ash reaches across and takes my hand, and I find a bit of strength in that.

'We know about the hacking,' Bennie is saying. 'We've seen the pictures and we know you were telling the truth. I'm sorry we doubted you, Honey. It's sick!'

'No, I'm sorry,' I say. 'It's driving me a little bit crazy, but . . . the worst of it was thinking I'd lost you guys. I think you're amazing, both of you. I've been miserable, thinking you hated me.'

Bennie grins. 'We don't do hate,' she says simply. 'Besides, it'd take more than a few silly words to wreck this friend-ship.'

'We're mates,' Tara chimes in. 'You're stuck with us.'

Seconds later, the three of us are clinging together in a clumsy, emotional hug. I break away briefly to drag Ash into it too, and we hang on tight and hold each other close, and a little bit of the pain inside me peels away.

Later, after I've showered and changed and combed my hair, we sit in the kitchen drinking ice-cold orange juice. Turns out that Ash went over to Willowbank at lunchtime to tell Tara and Bennie about yesterday, and how worried he was; the three of them have come straight from school, Ash arranging cover for his beach-cafe shift. I have friends who actually care about me, which is kind of amazing.

'We have to figure out who's doing this, and why,' Tara says. 'If the hacker really is Surfie16 and Surfie16 isn't Riley . . . then who? Do you have any enemies?'

'Looks like it,' I say. 'Lucky me, huh? I wondered about Liane, but I don't think she'd do this. Would she?'

'Don't think so,' Tara says. 'She's just a gossipy, spiteful girl – I think she's reacting to it all, but I don't think she's

❀❀❀❀❀❀❀❀❀❀❀❀❀❀❀❀❀❀❀❀❀❀

actually behind it. It has to be someone with a reason to lash out.'

'How about Cherry?' Bennie suggests. 'The stepsister from hell?'

I frown. I can't stand Cherry, but I cannot imagine her writing the toxic, hateful stuff of the last few days.

'There's a problem with that theory,' I say. 'She's several thousand miles away.'

Ash raises an eyebrow. 'We can't assume it's someone local,' he points out. 'Let's look at every possibility. Could someone have your password?'

I blink. I've had the same password for just about everything since I was thirteen and first had a SpiderWeb page. At Tanglewood we all knew each other's, because we shared a computer and people were always forgetting to logout. That puts Cherry in the frame again, of course.

'A few people know my password,' I admit. 'People back home. Look, if I had any ideas, I'd tell you, I swear . . . but I don't. Should I just ask Surfie16 outright?'

'No way,' Bennie says, eyes wide. 'He could be some kind of psycho, and he has your address, right? Honey, this is scary. Have you told your dad? Your mum?'

❀❀❀❀❀❀❀❀❀❀❀❀❀❀❀❀❀❀❀❀❀

'Dad wouldn't listen,' I say. 'And I don't want Mum to know – she'd be worried sick, and she's too far away to help.'

'Look,' Ash says. 'This is cyber-bullying. I bet your head teacher wouldn't stand for it. If you won't tell anyone else, tell her. Tell the police, tell *someone*!'

Is he right? Is speaking out the only way to stop this? I think of the damage this hate campaign has done, slicing right through my cool-girl mask to expose the scared little girl inside. I straighten my shoulders.

'I'll tell Birdie,' I agree. 'First thing tomorrow. I swear. And then I'll go to classes and face it all out, and if Liane or anybody dares to say anything to me –'

'We'll be with you,' Tara says. 'We'll meet you at the gates. Miss Bird is OK . . . she'll know what to do. Speak out, don't let this creep win!'

'Meanwhile,' Bennie says, 'Tara and I can report Surfie16 on SpiderWeb and report the spam on your page. It might take a day or two to go through, but they take things like this seriously.'

'Of course,' I say, wide-eyed. 'That should work. Thank you. Thank you!'

267

Long after they've gone, I lie in bed watching the moon-light dust the mirror shards in the window with silver. It's hot – stupidly hot. The TV news has been reporting bush fires for days, films of smoke clouds unfurling across the Blue Mountains, homes burnt to the ground. Logic and confidence fall away and fears crowd my head once more. My iPhone and laptop are broken, but the chances are that my stalker is still filling the Internet with hate. I try not to think of Dad's laptop, Emma's iPad, but I can't help myself. I want to know. I want to see. I want clues, truth, no matter how scary.

I get up and pad softly through the house to Dad's study.

Message:
Surfie16

What's the matter? Not answering my texts? I hope nothing's happened to your phone. It'd be awful if you lost it or broke it or got too scared to switch it on. But don't worry, Honey, I'll always find you. And there's always SpiderWeb, of course. I haven't finished with you yet.

BLUE ✿ ORCHID

24

I know I shouldn't try to confront Surfie16, but I cannot help myself. Do Australian teenagers lurk online at 5 a.m. the way he does? I don't think so. Maybe it's that he – or she – is in a whole different time zone.

I open up a new message and begin to type.

Who are you? Really?

A reply appears straight away.

Wouldn't you like to know? Perhaps someone you know pretty well . . . the person you least expect. And I'm going to destroy you, just like you destroyed me.

Just like that, my courage crumbles away and my head fills

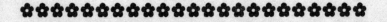

with doubts and fears. The person I least expect? Could it be Bennie or Tara? Or Ash? I log out again and snap the laptop shut, but now I'm back in the spider's web, trapped and helpless.

By morning, I have dredged up some strength and determination. Tara and Bennie will have reported Surfie16 by now, and though I am not looking forward to watching Birdie scroll through the nightmare of my SpiderWeb page, I am certain that telling her is the right thing to do. I am pretty sure she'll help.

Dad and Emma have left already, promising they'll be home on time later, pleased that I'm 'better' and returning to school. I wonder what they'd think if they bothered to actually listen, if they knew what I've been going through? Would they care? I bite my lip. I think they would, if I gave them a chance to.

My uniform is perfect, apart from the Converse; wearing one lone brown sandal is never a good look, but I'm hoping Birdie will understand and forgive me. I'm about to leave when the phone rings, and I drop my bag, silent, still. What if it's the stalker, if he's traced my landline somehow?

❁❁❁❁❁❁❁❁❁❁❁❁❁❁❁❁❁❁❁❁❁❁❁❁❁❁

And then I hear Skye's voice, small and faraway and wobbling slightly, on the answer machine.

'Honey, I need to talk to you. You won't answer your phone and you won't answer texts and I know you've been blocking us from SpiderWeb . . . now this!'

Answering the call will make me late for school, but I pick up the phone.

'Skye?' I say. 'It's me. Oh, it's so good to hear you!'

There's a silence, and the faint crackle and buzz of the line. As far as I can work out, it's around 10 p.m. back home, which is an odd time for Skye to be calling, but I am not complaining. Just hearing her voice makes me feel so homesick I could cry.

'Good to hear from me?' she says. 'What is wrong with you? How could you do this? How could you be so cruel?'

Dread seeps through me, cold and heavy.

'What are you talking about?'

'You know exactly what I mean,' Skye says. 'I was upset when you blocked us on SpiderWeb, but now I wish you'd left it that way. You're sick, Honey! What did we do to deserve this?'

272

❀❀❀❀❀❀❀❀❀❀❀❀❀❀❀❀❀❀❀❀❀❀❀

I glance around the kitchen, spy Emma's iPad and fold back the cover, still clutching the phone. Luckily, it's not locked and I log in to my home page; it looks the same as before. It's upsetting, obviously, but Skye's *What did we do to deserve this?* makes no sense.

'Skye, I have no idea what you're talking about,' I say. 'But if you've seen something bad, it's because my Spider-Web page has been hacked. Somebody's been blocking my friends and family, sending me threatening texts –'

Skye isn't even listening. 'Don't lie, Honey, it had to be you,' she says. 'Nobody else would have known how to hurt us so much!'

I click away from my home page and on to Skye's, recoiling as a series of graphic war images unfolds; death, injuries, mutilation. My stomach heaves.

'I can see,' I whisper. 'Oh God, I can see . . .'

'Why would you do this?' Skye repeats. 'I don't understand! We've tried to delete, but the pictures just keep coming back.'

I click to Cherry's page, spammed with pictures of horrible, violent manga; on Coco's, photos of sickening animal cruelty are everywhere. I'm crying by the time I get to

273

Summer's page, but the pictures there still make me flinch: images of morbidly obese women, of skeletal, starving children, each one supposedly posted by me.

Who would do such a thing? And who actually knows enough about my sisters to choose the images that would hurt the most? No wonder Skye thinks I am to blame.

'Summer is hysterical,' Skye is saying. 'She's shut herself in the bedroom, saying that she hates herself. You've ruined everything, Honey. How could you?'

I take a deep breath in. 'Is Mum there?' I ask. 'Can I speak to her?'

'She's out with Paddy,' Skye says, 'at a fortieth birthday party in Exeter. They're going to stay over. They don't know about this yet, but I'm going to tell them, Honey. You've gone too far this time!'

'Skye, listen,' I plead. 'Somebody has control of my SpiderWeb page. They've been trolling me for weeks. I've tried to delete my account but it just comes straight back. You have to believe me!'

'I don't know what to believe,' my sister says, and I wish with all my heart I didn't have a reputation as a rule-breaking drama queen who never lets the truth get in the way of a good night out, because maybe if I didn't she'd believe me now.

'I didn't do it,' I repeat. 'Take a look at my page and see what's on there.'

'We're still blocked,' Skye says. 'Are you lying to me, Honey?'

I think of the shattered mirror, the fragments of glass glinting in the window. I think of my laptop and mobile lying at the bottom of the swimming pool, of how this time yesterday I wanted to be at the bottom of the swimming pool too.

'I'm not lying, I swear,' I say. 'I thought I could contain it . . . sort it. I didn't want you to know I've messed up yet again. I didn't think anyone would believe me. I've told Dad, but he was tired and I didn't explain it properly and he didn't listen. I'm scared, Skye. Really scared.'

'It's really not you?' my sister asks.

'It's really, really not. I swear on my life.'

'So . . . what if we report your posts, tell SpiderWeb you've been hacked?' Skye suggests, and I don't know whether to laugh or cry. She believes me.

'Do that,' I reply. 'And have a think, Skye. I need to know

❀❀❀❀❀❀❀❀❀❀❀❀❀❀❀❀❀❀❀❀❀❀❀❀❀❀

who's doing this, who hates me so much they want to ruin everything I have – and lash out at the people I love most. It must be someone close to me, someone who knows me well.'

'I'll tell Mum as soon as she gets back tomorrow,' Skye says. 'She'll know what to do. We'll work it out, Honey, I promise.'

'I love you,' I tell my sister. 'And I'm sorry, Skye. For everything.'

I put the phone down, numb. Skye says Mum will be back in the morning, but 'morning' at Tanglewood is still ten or twelve hours away. I'm not sure I can survive that long. What made me think that coming to Australia would solve my problems? I carry my troubles with me wherever I go, an especially toxic kind of hand luggage. And if one set of problems gets sorted, I just conjure some more out of thin air.

It's a skill.

Right now, though, self-pity is fast being replaced with a slow, simmering rage. Tormenting me on SpiderWeb is one thing, but nobody, *nobody* touches my sisters. If I could see my stalker right now I would tear them to shreds, but

❀❀❀❀❀❀❀❀❀❀❀❀❀❀❀❀❀❀❀❀❀❀

of course, an Internet troll is sneaky and secretive, hiding behind a spider's web of lies and fakery. A weak person, a mean person, a cowardly person.

I want to throw chairs across the kitchen, smash plates, hammer my fists against the wall until they are raw and bloody, but none of that will help. I swallow back my fury and storm out of the house, but instead of turning towards school I head in the opposite direction. I walk towards town, and every step keeps me from screaming out loud at the nightmare that is my life.

All around me, people are going about their lives; I am detached from it all. I hold my head up high and keep walking, following signposts, asking directions, one foot in front of the other. It takes me over four hours to walk to Circular Quay, and by the time I get there I have blisters on my feet and sunburn on my nose. I buy a cold lemonade and walk up through the botanical gardens, retracing the path I took with Dad and Emma that very first day in Sydney when I still thought everything was going to work out.

Australia is beautiful, but I don't belong here . . . not now. I need to speak to Dad, make him listen and understand. I need to go home, to be with my mum and sisters – if they'll have me. Too late, I worry that 'last chance' could mean just that.

I recognize Dad's office block in the distance and walk right in through the revolving doors. I try not to meet the eyes of the business-suited men and women travelling skywards with me as I take the lift to the tenth floor, and when I get to reception, I ask to see Greg Tanberry.

The woman at the desk shakes her head. 'Sorry, you'll need an appointment; Mr Tanberry is out to lunch,' she says. 'I can book you in for next week, perhaps?'

I didn't think I might need an appointment to see my own dad, but hey, I'm way down on his list of priorities, I know that much. I am sick of waiting for Dad to see me, to listen to me, to notice I'm even alive. I could shout and yell and let the world know that my dad hasn't spared me more than an hour or two of his precious time and attention in years, but where would that get me?

'I *have* an appointment,' I say with authority. 'A lunch appointment, with my father. I assumed we'd be meeting here, but . . .'

The receptionist looks flustered, checking through her

❀❀❀❀❀❀❀❀❀❀❀❀❀❀❀❀❀❀❀

appointments book. 'I see. I'm so sorry. Well . . . there's nothing in the book, so perhaps you were meant to be meeting at the restaurant? I made a reservation for him, for one o'clock, at the Blue Orchid Bistro.'

It's past two by the time I get back down to Circular Quay. The Blue Orchid is one of those expensive places set right on the bay, and I see Dad the moment I step inside; he is in the corner, at a table for two, his back to me.

'Can I help you?' a waiter asks, frowning slightly at my blue school dress, my Converse, the look on my face as I push past. I see Dad lean forward, laughing, stroking the hand of his woman companion, feeding her forkfuls of dessert from his own plate. She's younger, of course – younger even than Emma. Her lips are painted scarlet and her dangly silver earrings shimmer as she leans forward, ruffling Dad's hair, trailing a finger along his jaw.

I feel angry for Emma, angry for Mum; but most of all, I feel angry for myself. Dad is not the person I thought he was – cool, charming, charismatic. He's a cheat. And he'll never change.

Dad's companion notices me staring, and her face

registers shock, worry. Then Dad turns, and I see a fleeting glimpse of pink stain his cheeks and wonder if that signifies shame or anger.

'Honey!' he says, fixing on his widest grin. 'What a lovely surprise! What brings you here?'

I shake my head, blinking back tears.

'I need your help, Dad,' I say. 'I need to talk to you, but I can see it's not a good time. I can see you're busy. I guess I'll just call the office and see if I can get an appointment.'

'Honey, don't be ridiculous,' Dad says. 'We'll talk later. Nothing's so urgent it won't keep, eh? I don't know what you're doing out of school, but I suggest you calm down and go back right now. This is a client meeting, obviously, but I'd rather you didn't mention it to Emma. She can be quite irrational –'

I laugh. 'That's funny,' I say, 'because I can be irrational too. Maybe Emma and I have more in common than I thought!'

I take the edge of the white tablecloth in my fingers, stroking the expensive handmade lace trim. And then I yank the whole thing towards me, scattering cutlery, dishes, glasses and condiments all over the shiny parquet floor.

'So. Nice to meet you,' I say to Dad's companion. 'Glad you got your earring back. Bye!'

I turn on my heel and walk out of the restaurant, picking my way carefully through the broken glass and china.

Hey Honey,

I waited at Willowbank for you this morning, but you didn't turn up and I had to go to class. Tara and Bennie say you weren't in all day, so I thought I'd call over, but you're not here. We're all worried sick about you.

I'll be at the cafe till 6 p.m., if you can get there?

Stay safe.

Ash xxx

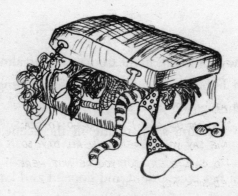

25

I take the bus home and call Mum from the landline, and when I hear her voice I fall to pieces. Skye has shown her the spammed SpiderWeb pages and told her what's been happening, and she doesn't doubt or blame or criticize, she just listens quietly and lets me spill it all out. I tell her everything, every sleazy detail, every spiteful status, every threatening text. I cry until there are no more tears left, and Mum listens and makes soft, soothing noises and tells me she loves me.

'I want to come home, Mum,' I whisper. 'I'm scared, and I want to come home.'

'It's OK, Honeybee,' Mum says. 'I'll sort it. I promise. Get packing.'

*

By the time Emma gets home from work, I'm almost done, shorts and T-shirts and crumpled dresses all flung into the case together.

'Honey?' Emma says, taking in the scene. 'What's going on?'

I look at her face, bright and hopeful and kind, and I wonder if she knows her whole life is a sham. My dad ruins everything he touches, just like me.

'Everything's wrong,' I say. 'I've been trying to tell you for days. Someone's hacking my iPhone and my laptop, threatening me, stalking me, turning everyone against me, even my own sisters! I have to go home, I want to go home . . . so I skipped school and went into town to see Dad, only he was out to lunch and when I got there . . .'

I shut my eyes, swallowing back more tears because it turns out that I am not all cried out after all, not yet.

'Oh, Emma,' I sob. 'He was with a woman. I think he's seeing her. I don't know if I should be telling you this . . . I don't know what to do!'

Emma puts her arms round me and holds me tight, stroking my hair as I cry, and we stay like that for a long time, until I am calm.

284

❁❁❁❁❁❁❁❁❁❁❁❁❁❁❁❁❁❁❁❁❁❁❁❁

'Shhh,' Emma says, taking my hand and leading me through to the kitchen. 'It's not the end of the world! We'll get this sorted, I promise you. We'll report the hacking, tell the authorities, find the culprit. I feel awful. I could see you weren't yourself, but I thought it was a flu bug. I had no idea. I've been a little preoccupied, and I should have seen . . . should have known something was wrong. I let you down, Honey.'

I blink, amazed. 'You didn't let me down, Emma,' I say. 'I should have trusted you, told you. But . . . didn't you hear what I said?'

'Of course!' she says, her smile a little too bright. 'If you want to go back to Somerset, then we can sort that too. You've coped amazingly well, Honey, but fifteen is very young to be apart from your mum and sisters.'

'Mum's going to sort a ticket,' I say. 'But that's not what I meant. Emma, what about Dad? Don't you understand? I saw him with another woman!'

Emma turns and strides into the kitchen, filling the kettle and ransacking the cupboard for teabags. 'Tea,' she says. 'Hot, sweet tea makes everything better, doesn't it?'

She sits down beside me, shoulders slumping.

❀❀❀❀❀❀❀❀❀❀❀❀❀❀❀❀❀❀❀❀❀❀

'I know about Greg,' she says. 'I've known for a while. The late nights, the phone calls. I know the signs.'

My eyes open wide. 'You . . . know the signs?' I echo. 'He's done it before?'

Emma laughs, but there's no humour in it. 'It's just Greg,' she says. 'It's what he's like. He's a good-looking man, and he thrives on attention. He's had flings before, but that's all they are. He loves me; he comes back to me. We have a good life here, a lovely house, nice holidays. It upsets me sometimes, of course it does, but why rock the boat over something like this?'

I can't believe what I'm hearing.

'Thing is, I haven't been a hundred per cent honest with you,' Emma says. 'Truth is, I *did* start seeing Greg when he was still married to your mum. I'm not proud of that, but Greg has a way of drawing people in, making them feel like they're the most important person in his universe . . .'

I nod. I know all about that. Dad reels people in with his charm and they glow golden under his attention: friends, family, business contacts, even shopkeepers, waiters, buskers in the street. He makes everyone special, just for a

286

moment or two, and then he moves on and we're left wondering what we did wrong.

Emma's eyes shine with tears. 'Your mum couldn't handle it,' she says. 'She finished things. But when Greg moved in with me, I knew what I was taking on. Men like Greg are hopeless, always falling for the latest conquest. But it never lasts. Why make a fuss? It's easier to ignore it, wait for it to pass.'

Her hands are shaking as she dabs at her eyes, leaving smudges of mascara across her perfectly powdered cheeks. The luxury lifestyle she's hanging on to looks thin and tawdry now, and Emma just seems lost, trying to tell herself everything's fine when clearly it isn't. As for Dad, he has let me down over and over; I can't pretend any more that it doesn't hurt.

'How *can* you forgive him?' I whisper. 'I don't understand! You say you don't want to rock the boat, but can't you see? It's all just lies!'

Emma is defensive now, distressed. 'You think I'm wrong to turn a blind eye?' she challenges. 'You think I'm stupid, weak? Even Charlotte forgave him the first time. She ignored his first fling, the one before me. Of

❀❀❀❀❀❀❀❀❀❀❀❀❀❀❀❀❀❀❀❀❀❀❀

course, she didn't know how serious it was, didn't know about the baby –'

She stops short, aghast. Her hand flies up to her mouth as if she can stop the words slipping out, but it's too late, of course. Way, way too late.

'What baby?' I say.

There's a silence. I can see Emma working out how to backtrack, but the secret is out and it can't be buried again, not now.

'Tell me,' I say, my voice cold, determined. 'You have to tell me everything.'

Emma bites her lip, then raises her chin and begins the story. 'It was a long time ago, back when you were a toddler,' she begins. 'The twins would have been babies, I think. The woman's name was Alison Cooke – I know because I worked for your dad back then and I helped to arrange a big financial pay-off for Alison, to look after the child in the years ahead. Greg wanted it all hushed up – he didn't want Charlotte to know. She was pregnant with Coco, if I recall.'

'This baby,' I ask, my head whirling with all of this information. 'Was it a girl or a boy?'

❀❀❀❀❀❀❀❀❀❀❀❀❀❀❀❀❀❀❀

'I never knew the details,' Emma admits. 'Alison lived in London, that's all I know. She started trying to contact Greg again two years ago, and he panicked, thought she must be looking for another payout. It was one of the reasons he took the Australian contract. He didn't want his past catching up with him.'

I'm stunned. This is Dad all over – one big disappearing act. I just never guessed how many secrets he's been hiding. He loves me, sure; he just isn't much of a father, or much of a man. He leaves a trail of destruction behind him, just as I seem to do.

Emma is sobbing now, afraid that Dad will be furious with her, and the roles reverse as I put my arms round her. I didn't want to share my dad with anyone, least of all the girlfriend who triggered his divorce from Mum, but Emma has never been anything other than kind to me. Right now, seeing her struggle to deny there's any problem with Dad's latest affair, all I can feel for her is pity.

I promise Emma I won't tell. It's an easy promise to make – right now, I don't much care if I never speak to Dad again.

I take my secret and go back to my packing, still

❀❀❀❀❀❀❀❀❀❀❀❀❀❀❀❀❀❀❀❀❀❀❀

shell-shocked, feeling the impact of it all unfurling inside me. Somehow it feels better to know the truth – it is easier to live with than a pipe dream of a happy-ever-after that can never happen.

Somehow, amazingly, I have a brother or sister, around the same age as Coco. As the idea settles, the initial shock and horror fade, replaced by a mixture of awe and hope. Dad may not want anything to do with this other family, but surely the rest of us have a right to know, maybe even get the chance to meet our half-sibling?

It's like finding a missing piece of jigsaw, the bit I need to complete the picture. A few months ago I couldn't see the picture at all; now I know that being a family is about much more than the names on a birth certificate. Maybe I can find Alison Cooke and trace my half-sister or brother; I will try my best to repair some of the damage Dad has done.

I slip my paintings carefully into the lid of the suitcase; the self-portraits are a visual diary of a girl in meltdown. I've been breaking apart and putting myself together again over and over, but finally I have stopped trying to re-make that perfect version of me that fell to pieces when

Dad walked away. It wasn't so perfect anyway, I know that now.

I am changing the pattern, changing my expectations, changing the story to make something new. It's like shedding a skin, and finding that the real me was there all the time.

I get to the beach cafe just as Ash is handing over to the evening shift. His face lights up and I run into his arms and hold on tight.

'Where were you?' he demands. 'I've been so worried! Tara and Bennie went to Miss Bird anyway, and she's going to investigate. She's sending a letter to your dad.'

'Good old Tara and Bennie,' I say.

Ash takes my hand and we walk out across the boardwalk and on to the dunes, and after a while we flop down on the sand, looking out towards the ocean.

'So,' Ash prompts, 'did something else happen?'

'I guess things stepped up a level,' I say. 'My sisters' SpiderWeb pages were spammed. I walked into town to talk to Dad –'

'Walked?' he echoes. 'It's, like, ten miles to the city centre!'

'I have blisters to prove it,' I say. 'I was angry. Walking helped. When I got there, they said I needed an appointment, but I blagged my way into the restaurant where Dad was having lunch and found him smooching with his mistress. Nice, huh?'

'Oh, Honey,' Ash sighs.

I squeeze his hand. 'I called Mum and talked to her about the hacking, and I told Emma I'd seen Dad with another woman. Emma got upset and told me some stuff she shouldn't have . . .'

'Like?'

'Like I have a half-brother or sister somewhere back home,' I say. 'My head's kind of all chewed up, just thinking about it. It seems like all this happened when I was a toddler, and Mum never knew. Dad just paid the woman off and hoped she'd go away. And then a while ago she got back in touch, and Dad panicked and took the Sydney job. He really is a great dad, huh?'

'Almost as good as mine,' Ash says. 'Cheats and runaways, both of them. I'm going to pretend my dad was some Hollywood star instead. Or a famous writer, or a rock star, or something. What d'you reckon?'

I laugh, and Ash says he'll take Johnny Depp and I pick out David Tennant because he seems cool, kind and has excellent time-travel skills.

'He'd fix this hacking mess, no problem,' I tell Ash. 'One zap of his Sonic Screwdriver and the troll gets blasted half-way across the universe. I wish. Although to be fair, I'm not as scared now people know about it. Mum and Paddy are on to it; so is Miss Bird, and Emma was threatening to ring the police. Tara and Bennie have reported it to Spider-Web and my sisters are sleuthing away trying to work out who the stalker might be.'

'SpiderWeb will tell you, once they've investigated,' Ash says. 'And if the police are involved, I expect he'll be pros-ecuted too. It's probably just some random creep who happened to hit on your SpiderWeb page by accident.'

'Maybe.' The thing is, I am pretty sure that Surfie16 is not a stranger. He knows too much about me, right down to exactly which images would freak out my sisters, and that means it's almost certainly someone back home. I think back to this morning's threat.

I'm going to destroy you, just like you destroyed me . . .

Who would even say that? It's not like I've had a

squeaky-clean past, but I have never set out to destroy anyone. What if it wasn't intentional, though? I feel dizzy for a moment as I think about the trail of hurt I've left behind me. There is someone . . . someone I hurt badly, used and threw away. The pieces fall into place. I know with a chill certainty exactly who has done all of this.

'You OK?' Ash is asking. 'You're miles away.'

I sigh. Miles away . . . that kind of sums it up.

'There's something I need to tell you, Ash,' I say. 'Thing is . . . I'm going back to England. Mum's sorting a ticket for me, and I think it might be quite soon. I am going to miss you so, so much.'

He folds his arms round me and holds me so tight that all the hurts melt away and all the broken pieces of my past fit together again. If only I could stay right here I'd be safe for always because Ash is the only boy I've ever met who can see past the cool-girl mask to the real me. He's the only boy who isn't afraid to stand up to me and tell me when I'm wrong, the only boy I'd actually listen to. He is kind and loyal and so drop-dead gorgeous he makes my insides melt, and I have to walk away from him. It breaks my heart.

We kiss for a long time while the sun goes down around us. My lips taste of salt, and I cannot tell if it's from my tears or his.

Quantas
<quantas@ausnet.com>
to me ✉

Thank you for your purchase. Your e-ticket and flight details are attached below. Thank you for choosing to fly with Quantas Airlines!

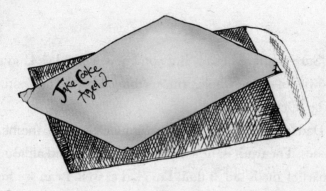

Jake Cooke aged 2

26

Saying goodbye is painful. Dad and Emma take me out to lunch and we talk about happy times; our hike in the Blue Mountains, our sightseeing day, Christmas Day at the beach. Anyone looking at us would think we were the perfect family, but I know better. We don't talk about the restaurant scene and we don't mention my failed new start and we definitely don't discuss the laptop and the iPhone at the bottom of the swimming pool; we act as if those things never happened at all, and I wonder what kind of life it would be, tiptoeing round the bad stuff, pretending you don't see it. It works for Dad, but I don't think it's working for Emma.

'OK, Princess?' Dad asks, ruffling my hair like I'm five years old. 'We've had some fun, haven't we, these last few months? Me and my best girl?'

'Sure we have,' I say. 'But you know what? I've kind of grown out of the whole princess thing. I got fed up waiting to be rescued.'

Dad frowns and goes back to his lunch, and the moment passes. The truth is, he's no longer my hero, and although a part of me is sad at that, I'm glad as well. I can see him for what he is now: weak, selfish, charming, destructive – exactly as I once was. Now I've worked out the stalking thing, I can see that clearly, and I'm not proud of it. I'm sorry that my own selfish actions could hurt someone so, push them right over the edge. Facing my stalker is one thing I am not looking forward to when I return home, but it's something that needs to be done.

What can I say? I'm trying to change. Dad never will, but I still love him, in spite of it all. Like I said, you don't get to choose who you love. Australia has been a learning process, and I am not talking about calculus or that experiment we had to do in science that made the whole lab stink of rotten eggs. I'm talking growing up, getting real, making friends, falling in love. Those things are worth crossing oceans to find.

I spend my last afternoon at the beach with Tara and

Bennie. We promise to meet up again one day, to travel the world and eat pizza at midnight and paint our toes turquoise and dance in the surf. Meanwhile, we'll write – proper letters because it'll be a while until I can trust SpiderWeb or the Internet again.

Saying goodbye to Ash is the hardest of all.

'I have a plan,' he says. 'I finish school in a few months' time and I'll come to the UK for my gap year, OK? To be with you.'

'I'll come back here one day too,' I promise. 'Go to art college, maybe, rent a little flat near the beach . . . if you want me to.'

'I want you to,' he says. 'You know I do.'

He dips into the pocket of his jeans and brings out a tiny twist of tissue paper. 'I saw this and thought you might like it. So you won't forget me . . .'

'I will never forget you,' I tell him. 'How could I? Besides, you're coming to Tanglewood in the summer. It's just a few months.'

I open up the tissue paper and inside there's a tiny silver honeybee charm on a soft cotton cord. Ash threads it round my neck, his fingers soft against my skin. We walk

299

barefoot along the shoreline under the stars and when we kiss, the waves wash in and out again around us, taking our sadness far out to sea, for a little while at least.

There is one last thing I have to do before I leave. Late at night, when Dad and Emma are asleep, I sneak into Dad's study and open up the laptop. I don't click on to SpiderWeb – my account has been suspended while their security team investigates. Instead, I search through Dad's online files and folders for something, anything, that might give me a clue to the past. There's nothing. Exasperated, I hunt through drawers, files, cupboards. I have almost given up when I find a small, locked briefcase, and although there's no key, I pick the lock with a hairpin, something Kes showed me once when his friend had shut his car keys inside the car.

The briefcase lock springs open, revealing a big brown envelope. My hands shake as I slide out a slim sheaf of papers; handwritten letters, a London address and a glossy photograph of a grinning toddler with dark blue eyes and messy fair hair. The child looks just like Coco at that age, and my hands shake as I turn the photo over.

❀❀❀❀❀❀❀❀❀❀❀❀❀❀❀❀❀❀❀❀❀❀❀❀❀

On the back, a name is written: *Jake Cooke, aged two*.

I have a brother.

Less than forty-eight hours later, I'm stepping off the plane at Heathrow into a cold, icy drizzle. Mum, Paddy and my sisters are waiting in Arrivals with one of Coco's home-made *Welcome* banners draped between them, and I run into Mum's arms and stay there a long time, holding tight.

I wish I could turn the clock back to when Dad left because now I understand what happened much better. Mum didn't want to hurt me; she stayed quiet, protected Dad, soaked up all the anger and blame I could throw at her and kept on loving me just the same. I even know the secret Dad never told, and I wonder how I'll ever find the courage to share it. I will, though, one day.

I hug my sisters in turn, even Cherry. Logic told me she had to be suspect number one in this whole stalking night-mare; she's the one person I set out to hurt, to drive away, yet instinct told me from the start that she would never do those things. I'm nowhere near the stage where I can forgive her for what happened with Shay, but I will try to be nicer to her from now on. Maybe.

❀❀❀❀❀❀❀❀❀❀❀❀❀❀❀❀❀❀❀❀❀❀❀

Back at Tanglewood, Mum lets us flop on the blue velvet sofas sipping hot chocolate while my sisters ask about a million questions, and I try to answer. I tell them about Tara and Bennie, about Ash and how he's going to visit in the summer, about Emma's kindness and Dad's bad temper and how I pulled the tablecloth out and smashed all the glass and china when I found him schmoozing with his latest fling.

'Poor Emma,' Mum says, and she really means it; she let go of the past and moved on long ago. I look at the life Mum's built with Paddy and I know in my heart it is better, stronger, happier than anything she shared with Dad. I can't begrudge her that, not any more.

'Yeah, poor Emma,' I say.

'Poor you too,' Coco says. 'Being stalked by a mad, bad Internet troll. There was me, getting all huffy because you'd stopped texting and messaging and blocked us from Spider-Web, and all the time you were being hacked! Why didn't you tell us?'

I sigh. 'I thought I could handle it, at first,' I say. 'And then it got so bad I didn't want anyone to see it, especially not you guys. He was clever too. He blocked you, deleted texts, did everything he could to turn my friends against me. I guess he really did hate me.'

'It's over now,' Mum says firmly. 'People do bad things sometimes, lose the plot, but he's getting help, it's being dealt with. Best to stay out of it.'

I can't stay out of it, of course. The stalking almost made me lose the plot too, and although I understand a little about why I was the target, there are still so many things I need to ask.

'I want to see him,' I say. 'Can you arrange it, do you think?'

'Are you sure it's a good idea?' Mum asks. 'After all that's happened?'

I shrug. 'I'm not sure, no. I just know it's something I have to do.'

There's a *For sale* sign outside the house, a pretty cottage on the edge of the village, the manicured lawns now white with frost. I am here, in spite of Mum's advice; and I'm alone because I need answers and I know that this is the only way I'll get them.

A woman opens the door, her face creased with worry. 'We've been expecting you,' she says. 'Come in. He's just so

303

sorry. And I can promise you it will never happen again. But please, please don't press charges. Charlotte and Paddy have been to talk to us already – we know what's been happening, and we are taking it seriously, very seriously indeed.'

She ushers me inside, and I see a familiar figure in the corner, staring at a blank computer screen. Anthony. He looks across, but cannot meet my eye.

'So,' he says eventually. 'How was Australia?'

'Awesome,' I reply. 'Life-changing, you could say . . .'

Anthony raises an eyebrow. 'Whatever.'

I clench my fists, fighting anger. 'I am stronger than you think, Anthony,' I say. 'It took me a while to work it out, but the clues were there all along. You're the cleverest person I know where computers are concerned. Clever enough to hack the school system and change my grades; clever enough to hack my SpiderWeb account, read my private journal, steal my pictures. And you've always known my password, of course. I think you helped me set it in the first place.'

'I wasn't clever enough,' he says. 'You worked it out in the end – I knew you would. And the trouble I was in over the school hacking was nothing compared to this. The

304

SpiderWeb admin team has banned me for life from all their social networks, with a threat of criminal prosecution if I break the ban.'

'Am I supposed to feel sorry for you?'

Anthony's face twists into a grimace. 'I don't want your pity, thanks. I've had enough of it to last me a lifetime.'

He picks up a box of pills and presses one out of the blister pack, swallowing it down with a sip of water. 'Everyone thinks I'm crazy,' he says. 'The doctor has given me tablets, set me up to go and see a shrink. Can you believe it?'

It's my turn to look away, embarrassed. Anthony was always sharp, smart, logical; he was the least crazy person I knew. He helped me with my homework and looked at me sometimes with sad, puppy-dog eyes, and I thought things would stay that way forever.

'Why did you do it, Anthony?' I ask.

'Why?' he echoes. 'Do you really have to ask? Every day you were posting pictures of your perfect life in Sydney, even brighter and better than the one you had before. I was still here, expelled from school, my parents barely talking to me. So . . . why d'you think?'

I remember those first few weeks in Sydney, how I tried

305

to post happy pictures to make it look as if life was great. Doesn't everybody do that on SpiderWeb?

'I saw you'd started a new account,' Anthony is saying. 'I didn't think you'd add me if I used my real profile, so I invented one. When I was Surfie16, you liked me. You flirted with me, cared about me. It was only on the Internet, I know. You thought I was someone else – it wasn't real. But it felt that way, for a little while. Then you spoilt it all by telling me about the sad, pathetic boy you knew back home. The boy who threw away everything for you – and you didn't even care. You said I was a *lovesick nobody*.'

'I didn't mean that,' I argue, but the truth is I did mean it, probably, at the time. I was like Dad, too wrapped up in myself to think how my actions might hurt others. Anthony wasn't even on my radar.

'I think the photo of you with your new boyfriend was the last straw,' Anthony says. 'You looked as if you hadn't a care in the world. I wanted to hurt you – smash up your lovely new life, spoil your friendships, turn your family against you. You ruined my life; I wanted to ruin yours.'

I blink. 'I've never needed much help to mess things up, you know that,' I say. 'Australia wasn't great, if you want the truth. My dad's a cheat and a liar, I missed my sisters like mad and school was awful. Then someone turned my friends against me, and it went from bad to worse. So, yeah . . . thanks for that, Anthony! I thought we were friends?'

He smiles, a cold, self-satisfied grin. In that moment I can see Anthony for what he is, a lost boy who has tipped over the edge into a very dark place, laughing as he pulls the wings off flies and poisoned by his own self-pity. It's scary.

'We were never friends,' he snaps. 'You treated me like dirt on your shoe, so why the surprise when I did the same to you?'

I thought I was here to confront Anthony, to make him confess and show him he hasn't beaten me, but Anthony isn't playing the game. Instead, he is forcing me to look at the way I treated him, to see the damage I did. He's right – whatever we shared, it wasn't friendship. My past selfishness has come back to haunt me.

Anthony's mum comes in with a tray of tea, and his anger shuts down as suddenly as it appeared. My hands shake as I take my mug and listen as she tells me they are moving soon, up to the Midlands, that when Anthony is well again they'll help him to finish his schooling, go to university, build a future.

✿✿✿✿✿✿✿✿✿✿✿✿✿✿✿✿✿✿✿✿✿✿✿

'As long as you don't press charges,' she says. 'That would finish him. We'll make sure it doesn't happen again. He'll have no Internet, no access to computers.' She shows me the electrical lead to the PC Anthony is staring at, the plug chopped off.

It's hard to think of Anthony as a monster. It's hard to imagine how much he wanted to hurt me, how love turned to hate, but that's what happened, and I have to take a share of the blame. I used him. I saw that he liked me and reeled him in, kept him dangling like a puppet on a string. I caused real damage and hurt, and I'm not proud of that.

'I'm sorry, Anthony,' I say at last. 'I'm sorry for hurting you, using you. I didn't realize at first; I didn't understand, didn't think how it might feel to be you.'

He shrugs and turns away, back to staring at the blank screen. As Anthony's mum shows me out, her polite, anxious mask slips and I see cold blame in her eyes. I wish I could rinse that away.

Tanglewood wraps itself around me, and life goes on, the same but different. Coco is more grown-up, inches taller, riding Caramel and helping out at the stables in return for free lessons. Skye has a new hobby making feathered head-bands and Summer is totally loved up after a surprise birthday trip to the ballet with Alfie.

As for Paddy, his chocolates are on the shelves of a national department store, getting great press coverage for being fairly traded and ethical as well as wickedly tasty. Paddy's not my dad and never will be, but I've stopped blaming him for that – he makes Mum happy. We have a long way to go, but we're trying, and guess what, I am trying with Cherry too. It's early days, but hey, it's a start.

Any plans of idling the next few months away bite the dust when Mum takes me to see a sixth-form college the other side of Minehead, where they agree to let me take art and English and French GCSE this June, then start A levels after the summer. Before long, I'm back on a strict study timetable; Ash would be proud.

I've talked a lot with Mum about what happened when Dad left. She chose not to tell us that Dad had been having affairs ever since I was tiny; she didn't talk about the times he went missing for days, his selfishness, his temper, the endless rows when we were all tucked up safely in bed. 'That was between the two of us,' she says. 'Greg is a long way from perfect, but he loves you. He loves you as much as he can – remember that.'

It's too bad that it turned out not to be enough.

A few days back I found the old plastic tiara I used to wear for dressing up when I was a kid, back when I dreamt of being a princess. I threw it in the bin; there were too many unhappy memories. I think I've finally outgrown the princess phase. Maybe I should thank Dad and Anthony for what they've put me through because I survived, and I feel better, stronger, more hopeful now. I just wish it hadn't been such a bumpy ride.

So . . . how do you start again? You shake things up, blot everything out, let the snow settle. It's March now, and it's snowing at Tanglewood, the kind of quick, swirling storm that blows up from nowhere and vanishes again just as fast. When the snow settles, everything looks perfect, just like the snow globe I got for Christmas. I know it won't last for long, but that's OK. I'm not looking for perfect any more. I'm looking for reality because mixed up with all its hurts and hardships and disappointments there are moments of pure happiness and wonder, moments when it's all worthwhile. I curl up on the window seat of my turret room, reading a letter from Ash,

❀❀❀❀❀❀❀❀❀❀❀❀❀❀❀❀❀❀❀❀❀❀

pages of handwritten words that weave together to make a picture so real I can almost touch it, taste it. I think of a brown-eyed boy sitting in the sunshine, half a world away, and I know somehow that one day we'll be together again and that will be as close to perfect as I can imagine.

I put the letter down and pick up my own pen. I've been writing to Ash, Bennie and Tara regularly, but there's another, more important letter I've been meaning to write. I smooth out a clean sheet of paper, frowning.

What do you say? How do you begin? I have messed up so badly, for so long. I have hurt my family, done almost as much damage as Dad. There is one person I haven't messed up with, though. I can still redeem myself, reach out to my brother, let him know he isn't alone. I have learnt a lot about families, and though it's a big risk, I am almost sure that Mum and Paddy and my sisters will understand why this is something I have to do.

I am not sure how to begin, how to say the things I want to say, but I take a deep breath and begin anyway.

Dear Jake . . .

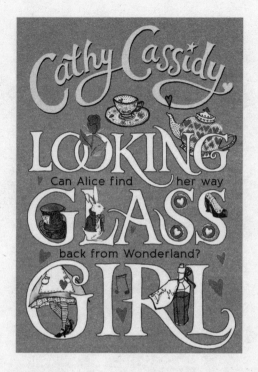

Look out for the next special treat from
Cathy . . . *Looking Glass Girl*.

Alice nearly didn't to go the sleepover. Why would Savvy, queen
of the school, invite someone like *her*?

Now Alice is lying unconcious in a hospital bed.

Lost in a world of dreams and half-formed memories, she is
surrounded by voices – the doctor, her worried friends and Luke,
whose kisses the night of the fall took her by surprise . . .

When the accident happened, her world vanished – can Alice
ever find her way back from wonderland?

Turn over for a sneak peek . . .

'Emergency, which service?'

'We need an ambulance! Please, quickly!'

'I am transferring you now . . .'

'Hello, you are through to the ambulance service. How can I help you?'

'We need an ambulance, like, now! My friend has fallen and she's not moving and I think she might . . . Look, we just need an ambulance, OK?'

'Where are you? Can you give me the address?'

'No! Oh, please, don't tell her, Yaz! I'm going to be in SO much trouble!'

'We're all going to be in so much trouble. That doesn't matter right now . . . I have to tell her, Savvy – how else is the ambulance going to get here?'

'The address?'

'Hello? Sorry. We need an ambulance to 118 Laburnum

❀❀❀❀❀❀❀❀❀❀❀❀❀❀❀❀❀❀❀❀❀

Drive, Ardenley. You have to hurry! She's fallen and she's not moving . . .'

'She's not moving at all? Where did she fall from?'

'She fell down the stairs. It was an accident!'

'Have you moved her?'

'No, we're scared to – she's lying all funny. She's just not moving. And there's all this broken glass and blood . . .'

'An ambulance is on its way to you now.'

'How long will it take? I'm so scared . . .'

'I need you to stay on the line. We'll be with you as soon as we possibly can.'

'It was an accident!'

'What is your friend's name?'

'Alice. Alice Beech . . .'

❀❀❀❀❀❀❀❀❀❀❀❀❀❀❀❀❀❀❀❀❀

2

Alice

'Can you hear me, Alice? My name is Martin. I'm a paramedic. Hang on, Alice . . .'

Everything is dark, the kind of thick, soft darkness that wraps around you like a blanket of sleep. I can hear someone talking to me, but I don't understand what he's saying – it's like some kind of secret code. It makes no sense at all.

'I'm calling in to report a head-trauma victim: female, age thirteen . . . We're blue lighting her . . .'

Head-trauma victim?

A shrill siren wail starts to screech, scratching its fingernails against my skin, filling up my senses. It makes everything hurt, but I can't seem to find the words to tell them to shut it up.

And suddenly I find myself falling backwards, down the rabbit hole,

dropping like a stone, my screams swallowed up by the soft blanket of darkness.

Year Six

I wasn't always a victim. Not so long ago, I was just a normal girl, a happy girl. I didn't get top grades in class and I wasn't the most popular kid in the school, but I had amazing friends and a happy family. I worried about all the usual things: test results, playground tiffs, whether I'd ever find a hobby I could be good at, something where I'd shine . . . but those worries never stopped me having fun.

And then, in Year Six, I was picked to play the lead role in our class production of *Alice in Wonderland*. It was only a school play in a draughty gym hall, but the audience whooped and whistled and stamped their feet, and I swished my sticky-out blue skirt and dropped into a curtsey, smiling so much it made my face ache. I don't think I'd ever been so happy.

My best friends, Elaine and Yazmina, only had small, non-speaking parts as two of the playing-card soldiers, but they were really pleased for me all the same.

'You were brilliant,' Yaz said. 'I could never have remembered all those lines!'

'And you got to do all those rehearsals with Luke Miller,' Elaine sighed. 'Lucky you! He's so cute!'

I laughed, but I wasn't crushing on Luke Miller like Elaine

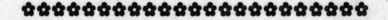

was. I'd known him since Reception Class and I saw him as a friend – annoying sometimes but good fun as well. It had been fun working on the play with him, but Luke was going to Ardenley Academy after the holidays, so I knew I wouldn't see him again. Elaine, Yaz and I were all going to St Elizabeth's, a strict, all-girls school that was supposed to get great results.

I actually wished the whole lot of us were going to Ardenley Academy instead; we'd been to look at St Elizabeth's, and I'd hated the gloomy, dark-panelled wood, the polished floors, the framed photographs of hockey and netball teams from years gone by that lined the corridor walls. I couldn't imagine spending the next seven years of my life in a place like that, wearing a braid-trimmed blazer and a grey pleated skirt and knee-length white socks. I mean . . . socks? Really? Not good. But Elaine and Yaz were both going there, so I buried my misgivings and signed up for it, and my parents were as proud as if I'd just passed half a dozen A levels with A* grades.

We finished Year Six on a high. Elaine, Yaz and I had mapped out our summer, planning sleepovers, picnics in the park, days out in town, backyard sunbathing sessions, but on the last day of term Miss Harper turned all of that upside down. She handed me a flyer about a drama summer school, and that changed everything.

'It's two days a week throughout the holidays,' she told me. 'A mix of kids, aged eleven to sixteen, all with a talent for acting. I thought that you and Luke would be perfect for it!'

I was so thrilled at being chosen that I didn't even notice the flickers of disapproval on the faces of my friends. I didn't notice it until two weeks later, when I was at Elaine's house for a sleepover. I was talking about an improvization exercise I'd done that day in drama with Luke Miller when Yaz interrupted me.

'Alice?' she said. 'No offence, but we're sick of hearing about your stupid drama club the whole time. And about Luke and what great mates you are these days. It's all you ever talk about, and it's getting boring.'

Elaine frowned. 'I know you don't mean it,' she said. 'But it's like you're rubbing our noses in it . . .'

I blinked. Was I talking too much about drama club? About Luke? Did it sound like showing off? Maybe.

'Sorry,' I said. 'I suppose I do get carried away, sometimes. It's just that it's so much fun, and I know you'd absolutely love it, and . . .'

Yaz and Elaine exchanged an exasperated glance, and my words trailed away to nothing.

'It was just a fluke that they gave you that part,' Yaz said. 'I bet Miss Harper just thought of you because your name was Alice, and decided to give you a chance . . .'

'Anyone can act,' Elaine agreed. 'If we went to special lessons, we'd be good too. But who wants all that stuff, anyway? Dressing up and playing games of Let's Pretend. I really didn't think Luke would go for that sort of thing. It's so *babyish*!'

After that, I was careful not to mention the drama classes, or Luke. I kept my mouth closed and tried hard to be interested when they talked about boys and make-up and music, but it knocked my confidence. Yaz and Elaine had never told me I was boring or babyish before; I'd thought they were happy I'd finally found something I was good at.

Instead of finding something cool to talk about when we were together, I was silent, anxious about saying the wrong thing. Yaz and Elaine began mentioning days out in town without me, a trip to the ice rink, a train ride down to the seaside. I tried not to mind. I was going to drama club without them for two days a week, so I could hardly complain if they did things without me, but for the first time ever I began to feel as if they were deliberately excluding me.

The summer turned sour. Sometimes, when I rang Yaz or Elaine, they were out . . . at the cinema, or down at the park, or just 'out'. Often, they forgot to ring me back. Maybe we'd been drifting apart, just a little, over the last year. Yaz and Elaine had sometimes rolled their eyes when I failed to summon up much interest in boy bands and crushes and turquoise nail varnish, but I hadn't thought those differences were fatal. I assumed we could find our way through them, like we always had before when one of us hadn't shared the others' passion for ballet or ponies or Harry Potter. I thought it would all blow over, but when they had a sleepover the last weekend of the holidays and didn't invite me, it didn't feel that way.

We were supposed to start at St Elizabeth's together, the three of us against the world. Instead I pulled on my new uniform, complete with socks and braided blazer, and walked to school alone because they hadn't answered my texts. Without my friends, I was struggling to keep my head above water in a sea of uniformed strangers. I was adrift, lost.

I wanted to cry and yell and run away home, but you don't do those things when you're eleven. You tilt your chin and bite your lip and pretend you don't care.

St Elizabeth's did its best to keep groups of friends together, and I was put in the same class as Yaz and Elaine. My face lit up when I saw them, and they smiled too, and for a moment I thought everything could still be OK for us.

'Hey, Alice,' Yaz said. 'How are you? We haven't seen you for weeks! How was your summer? How was that amazing drama club of yours?'

'It was great,' I said.

'I bet you made some cool new friends,' Elaine said.

'Well . . . a couple. They're all different ages, though, and I'm not sure any of them are at St Elizabeth's . . .'

'That's good, though,' Yaz told me. 'Meeting new people. Because we just haven't been on the same wavelength for a while now, have we?'

I bit my lip. 'Are you saying we're not friends any more?' I dared to ask.

'Of course we're friends,' Elaine said. 'Obviously we are!

But that doesn't mean we have to be in each other's pockets all the time, does it? We should make new mates, see other people. We're growing up, moving in different directions . . . Maybe we just need some space?'

Space? I'd heard that line before, back when Elaine's mum left her dad. 'She just needs some space,' Elaine had said. 'They'll probably get back together. Maybe. Most marriages need that, just to stay healthy. Your parents should probably do it too . . . They might just be staying together for you and Nathan.'

'I don't think so,' I said, and Elaine's face had twisted up, making her look bitter and angry. I knew how sad she was feeling inside, so I didn't go on about Mum and Dad being happy; I didn't want to make her feel worse than she did already.

Elaine's parents never did get back together. Elaine's mum found herself someone new, a boyfriend called Kevin with no job and an attitude problem. He made Elaine's life a misery.

And now Elaine wanted some space herself – from me.

'We're still friends,' Yaz clarified. 'But things are different now, Alice. Let's enjoy secondary school. New starts, new challenges, new friends. Best of luck!'

They walked away and left me alone.

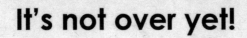

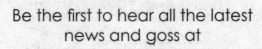

♥ Is your *best friend* one in a million?

♥ Is she always there for you — in the *good times* and the *bad*?

♥ Does she make you *happy* and make you *laugh*?

Well, now you can show your *best friend* how much she means to you . . .

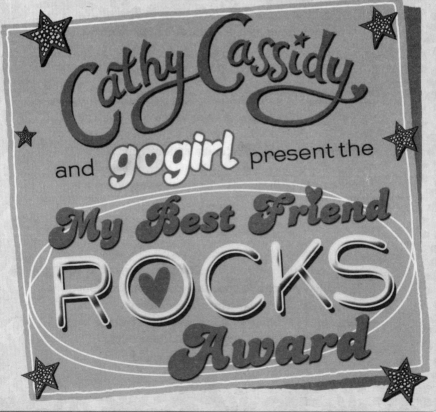

Cathy Cassidy and gogirl present the

My Best Friend ROCKS Award

It all started with a Scarecrow

Puffin is over seventy years old.
Sounds ancient, doesn't it? But Puffin has never been
so lively. We're always on the lookout for the next big
idea, which is how it began all those years ago.

Penguin Books was a big idea from the mind of
a man called Allen Lane, who in 1935 invented
the quality paperback and changed the world.
**And from great Penguins, great Puffins grew,
changing the face of children's books forever.**

The first four Puffin Picture Books were hatched in 1940 and the
first Puffin story book featured a man with broomstick arms called
Worzel Gummidge. In 1967 Kaye Webb, Puffin Editor, started the
Puffin Club, promising to **'make children into readers'**.
She kept that promise and over 200,000 children became devoted
Puffineers through their quarterly instalments of *Puffin Post*.

Many years from now, we hope you'll look back and
remember Puffin with a smile. **No matter what your age
or what you're into, there's a Puffin for everyone.**
The possibilities are endless, but one thing is for sure:
whether it's a picture book or a paperback, a sticker book
or a hardback, **if it's got that little Puffin
on it – it's bound to be good.**

www.puffinbooks.com